The Divorce

The Divorce

·

CÉSAR AIRA

translated by Chris Andrews

*with an introduction
by Patti Smith*

A NEW DIRECTIONS PAPERBOOK ORIGINAL

Originally published by Editorial Mansalva, Buenos Aires, as *El Divorcio* in 2010;
published in conjunction with the Literary Agency Michael Gaeb/Berlin

Manufactured in the United States of America
First published as a New Directions Paperbook (NDP1501) in 2021
Design by Erik Rieselbach

Library of Congress Cataloging-in-Publication Data
Names: Aira, César, 1949– author. | Andrews, Chris, 1962– translator. |
Smith, Patti, writer of introduction.
Title: The divorce / César Aira ; translated by Chris Andrews ;
with an introduction by Patti Smith.
Other titles: Divorcio. English
Description: New York : New Directions Publishing Corporation, 2021.
Identifiers: LCCN 2021001819 | ISBN 9780811230933 (paperback ; acid-free paper) |
ISBN 9780811230940 (ebook)
Classification: LCC PQ7798.1.17 D5813 2021 | DDC 863/.64—dc23
LC record available at https://lccn.loc.gov/2021001819

10 9 8 7 6

New Directions Books are published for James Laughlin
by New Directions Publishing Corporation
80 Eighth Avenue, New York 10011

A Kind of Introduction

I HAD SOME TREPIDATION ABOUT ACCEPTING THIS task: in truth, I felt a bit like Zelig, popping up yet again in César Aira's realm—first in the form of a blurb, and then with a book review, and now writing a kind of introduction, albeit a small one. But the personal upside would be to win such a trifecta of admiration for a beloved and deserving writer. Unlike this marvelous work's title (indicating a profound disassociation), nothing could please me more than the unique privilege of being associated with the cosmically mischievous and profound mind of César Aira.

I first collided with the author some time ago at a benevolently pristine literary festival in Denmark. I accosted him on a pathway and rambunctiously declared his book *An Episode in the Life of a Landscape Painter* a masterpiece, which he flatly denied. It was inexcusable of me, stopping the writer in his tracks to single out one novella within his prolific body of work, but the book had so beguiled me that I could not contain myself.

It wasn't until I read and reviewed *The Musical Brain* that I realized why he'd been so cavalier about the merits of the book that I had fervently pedestaled. César Aira is gifted with a vastly flexible, kaleidoscopic mind: he can see the equation and the proofs simultaneously. He sets one crystal in place and a whole structure manifests. Reading the many tales in *The Musical Brain,* it became clear that the qualities I had so admired in *An Episode* were commonplace to his process: just something he does. He draws you—by a tap on the shoulder or by the scruff of your neck—into a cascading nightmare, filled with a brightness you cannot resist entering.

Which brings me to the genesis of the task at hand. It was mid-April, at the height of the pandemic in New York City, and I was sitting at my desk before the blank pages of my journal when the doorbell rang. I had been thinking of emptiness. I was thinking about how millions of the faithful would be denied the pilgrimage to Mecca. I was thinking of ghost towns and empty cathedrals and empty opera houses and empty playgrounds and the empty apartments of my COVID-fled neighbors.

I fitted my mask, opened the door, and there at the top of my stoop was a cloth bag. I looked around just in time to receive a wave from my masked benefactor heading uptown on an old-fashioned bicycle. The bag, which had been sanitized, was filled with books and a slim, innocent-looking galley. Seeing that it was a new work of César's, I bounded up the stairs, pushed my work aside and began reading so hastily that I failed to remove my mask. The musical brain eats the keys, I mused, conscious that with César's new book in hand I would most likely not get my own work done.

As I read *The Divorce* it started to snow. By page seven I was drawn from the pandemic emptiness into a world filled to the brim, where rooms are overflowing, as are mirror images of the rooms, as are multiple reflections, and reflections of reflections of projections of the rooms. I read as the April snow continued to fall. I read on and on, in tandem with the sudden spreading of full sun, dissolving that unexpected blanket of white. Needless to say, as I read the last words, I melted.

It is not my desire to spoil things for the reader by attempting to pin down the plot but let me offer some small selected sentences, scattered jewels from the sections I'll call *fire, evolution club, manual,* and *ice.*

> FIRE: *It had been a meeting and a parting in one, precipitated by an accident or an adventure that, over time, had grown in their memories, taking on cosmic proportions, like a galactic explosion.*

> EVOLUTION CLUB: *There was nothing inside, except for an almost invisible object.*

> MANUAL: *That would have explained the hollow mother-of-pearl stars that kept brushing her forehead, supported by nothing, like real stars.*

> ICE: *The ice of Heaven was no less dangerous.*

In the section I call the *manual* a search is on for an enigmatic handbook filled with all the necessary instructions to fulfill a certain occupation's simplest duties. In a parallel fashion, *The*

Divorce itself outlines the process for those wishing to comprehend or to experience the expansive possibilities of a single moment. That is his wondrous gift, and *The Divorce* is the personification of that gift.

I am writing these words at my desk, having been transformed by the work of another. Suddenly, I have new goals, and a plan to transform my own room, with its dusty skylight and piles of books and talismans, into the energized space of the book's Evolution Club.

The wheel is turning. The wheel is the contained life of the book. Each spoke is an episode or a character. All are part of the same story, hitting the ground at different moments, setting off vibrations at various frequencies, created by whichever spoke or section of a spoke is the most prevalent at any given moment. Everything happens simultaneously. The empty frame contains a multitude of images: the end of sleep, the epic dream, the projection of the day ahead, the memory of the night before. All in the blink of an eye—and it's up to the writer to break it down, with incredible stamina, spoke by spoke, and give us a story.

His book is his own. Nothing said here could truly add to the smallest effort from the master himself. César Aira is a psychedelic geometer, and it is certain that *The Divorce* will leave you breathless, and that is all I have left to say.

—PATTI SMITH
OCTOBER 2020

THE DIVORCE

WHEN I LEFT PROVIDENCE (RHODE ISLAND) IN EARLY December, the first fall of snow already lay buried beneath the second, and the second fall beneath the third. I didn't care what Henriette's mother said, or the child psychologist at her kindergarten. It would be easier for her to accept my absence for a whole month than to have me show up on the doorstep of what had once been our house, knocking at the door like a stranger on Christmas morning or Boxing Day or Christmas Eve, after calling to make and confirm the arrangements, not to mention the parting that would have to follow. The divorce was still recent, and a new routine was gradually and painfully taking shape. I didn't feel ready, in my new situation, to face the season's cloying formalities. A temporary withdrawal on my part would be the kindest thing, for me and for my daughter. When I returned, all smiles and gifts, we would reestablish our relationship on the terms laid down by the judge.

This, in revised and summary form, is what I was saying to myself as the plane took off. What the explanation doesn't convey, with its clear and reasonable wording, is the emotional turmoil that I had been going through for months, or the crisis that had led to my departure. Those feelings began to wane as the summer days went by in the beautiful city that I had

3

chosen as the destination for my break. In the absence of significant others, I had the liberating sensation of being absent from myself. Sunny and rainy days alternated within a changeless continuum of light, a light that was always fine and delicate, touching things with fingertips, and lingering.... This impression might have been caused by the lengthy evenings, and the leaves on the trees, whose high branches met over the streets, and the air washed clean by daily showers.

I had chosen Buenos Aires almost by accident: I wanted to go somewhere far away and with completely different weather; it was the only city I could think of that satisfied both conditions and in which I had acquaintances. I called them before traveling. Although I didn't know them well, and hadn't even met some of them in person, they swung into action and came to my aid with the hospitality so characteristic of those latitudes. They arranged my accommodation, and soon after arriving I had settled into a pleasant guest house in a neighborhood that was so quiet and yet so full of attractions that I felt no need or desire to leave it during my stay. I was grateful for that practical help, of course, but even more so—and I reaffirm my gratitude here, in these pages—for the company, the conversation, the time those people spent with me.

Habits of leisure and relaxed sociability, without any discernible goal and all the more charming for their transience, established themselves within a few days. They were habits in the full sense of the word, as placid and reassuring as any others, but without that aftertaste of life imprisonment that habits generally have. The most regular—and in a way it included all the rest—was the habit of conversing at a sidewalk table belonging to one of the numerous cafés in the neighborhood.

One morning it so happened that I was at a table outside El Gallego, chatting with a young woman named Leticia, a talented video artist I had met two nights earlier at a dinner in the same establishment. El Gallego was a charming little restaurant, run by its founder, owner and driving force, an old Spanish immigrant who had always been known simply as El Gallego. When lunch and dinner weren't being served and even when they were, since the place was run in a fairly informal manner, it functioned as a café, bar and club for a varied local clientele, which I had been able to join without difficulty.

At one point we saw El Gallego himself come out onto the sidewalk. He was a tiny man; an inch shorter and he would have been a dwarf. In spite of his eighty years, he was still very active and in excellent physical condition. And I knew from my conversations with him that he was as mentally sharp as ever. The previous night, after saying goodbye to my dinner companions (they were heading home; my guest house was just around the corner—I didn't even have to cross the road), I had stayed on, talking with him over a last drink until the small hours of the morning.

He came out onto the sidewalk, with his quick step and his purposeful air, to extend the canvas awning in front of the restaurant. At that time of day, nearly noon, the sun shone through a gap in the foliage, and a blinding band of light was advancing toward the tables and their occupants. Like a benevolent spirit, forever mindful of his customers' comfort, El Gallego would not let anything bother us.

Absorbed in conversation with my young friend, I didn't notice his presence until the incident occurred. It all happened quickly. As soon as El Gallego inserted the crank handle and started turning it, and the first fold of the awning opened out, a mass of water fell onto the sidewalk. It had rained overnight and the water had pooled in the canvas. Luckily it came down well away from the line of tables, and didn't even splash us. Perhaps it wouldn't have splashed us even if we had been closer, because it was as if every last drop had been absorbed by the victim: a young man with a bicycle. He wasn't riding his bicycle but wheeling it; he had probably just gotten off and stepped up onto the sidewalk. The water doused him as if it had been expertly aimed. And it was no small amount. No shower of separate drops. It was a solid bucketful, gallons of it plunging with the force of gravity, right down onto him.

He stood there transfixed by surprise, fright, and wetness. Especially wetness, which overpowered all the rest. He was drenched, down to the last thread of his clothes, the last strand of his hair and the last cell of his skin. He seemed to go on getting wetter, in a process that transcended the temporality of the accident. The water ran over his face and down his arms (eddying around his watch); smooth waves of it passed under his T-shirt, swelling and rippling the fabric; it flowed down inside his Bermuda shorts, formed little translucent curtains like glass tubes around his calves, and bubbled coldly all over his sandaled feet.

We stared in fascination, frozen like him. He was right there in front of our table. A moment passed, the briefest of moments, perhaps. Time is especially hard to measure in such circumstances. Perhaps no time passed at all, or only the infinitesimal fraction of a second required for the eye of the totally soaked young man to communicate with his brain. He didn't have to look around because chance, as I said, had put him right there in front of our table; the same chance that had placed him beneath that cascade at just the right moment. He opened his mouth, parting the veils of water that were still flowing over his lips, and cried:

"Leticia!"

The young video artist who was sitting with me and had seen it all happen, suddenly found herself having to make a psychological readjustment. I know, because I was looking at her and could see the mental process reflected in her face. The protagonist of this episode had been a stranger, like every victim of a mishap witnessed in the street. It's never Juan or Pedro but the guy who tripped or was mugged or got run over. But now, with the help of memory, she had to reassign the stranger to the category of people whose names she knew. This too was a very rapid operation. It happened in a flash, before all the water had fallen from the awning, or so it seemed:

"Enrique!"

She leaped up, went straight over and hugged him, oblivious to getting wet. Then they stepped back to take each other in, to finish recognizing one another, after all that time.

THEY HADN'T SEEN EACH OTHER SINCE THE DAY THEY met, which was also the day that had marked the end of their childhood. It had been a meeting and a parting in one, precipitated by an accident or an adventure that, over time, had grown in their memories, taking on cosmic proportions, like a galactic explosion. That day was in fact a night, and only a brief part of a night, lasting perhaps just a few minutes, but so charged with entropic force that it remained indelibly etched. The incident had occurred fifteen years earlier, and could have left each of them with the impression that the other was an imaginary being, a figment of panic or of some obscure survival mechanism. Yet both of them had persisted in the belief that the other was real, and in something like the hope of recovering that reality … And now, suddenly, there they were, Leticia and Enrique, in the flesh, looking into each other's eyes. The reunion was amazing not only because of the absurd circumstances in which it had occurred, but also because of its material cause: water. The water enveloping Enrique's body, still flowing over him … As it happened, the cause of their first meeting and subsequent parting had been a fire. It was as if Destiny were working with primordial blocks. Fire had separated them; and now water had brought them together. Taking air for granted, or keeping it in reserve for a later stage of their shared story, all they needed to complete the classic quartet of the elements was the "earth, swallow me up" of unexpected and unwelcome encounters. But this encounter, so unexpected, was by no means unwelcome to either of them. On the contrary: what they were experiencing in that moment was something like the blessed consummation of memory made real. They were real, and had been real at the time of the College fire.

When the sun had risen the following day, a handful of ashes was all that remained of what had been an elegant and progressive boarding school on the outskirts of Buenos Aires, run on European lines, in accordance with the pedagogical theories of a German theosophist. The emphasis was on developing individual autonomy through crafts, proximity to nature, and spiritual development. An expertly balanced blend of primitivism and advanced technology promised to build characters that would ensure professional and social success as well as respect for the fundamental values of life. At the core of the whole concern was representation, the emblem and fulfilment of which was the building that housed the institution. Modeled on the mansions of Victorian England, with the same combination of the neo-Gothic and the grandiose, it was a sturdy and rather imposing pile with its bow windows, towers, and domes standing all alone in the middle of a vast, wooded park that contained a lake, tree-lined avenues, a rose garden, statues, and playing fields. When Enrique first entered the College (he had just turned thirteen), he felt as if he were stepping into a fairy-tale castle that was also a never-ending labyrinth; and he had not come to the end of it when, some months later, in the middle of winter, it burned down.

To the puzzlement of the expert investigators called in by the insurance company, the fire began simultaneously at various places in the College, on different floors and in different wings of the building, which measured a hundred meters across the facade and extended back almost as far, while the towers were thirty meters high. To the left and right, up on the balconies and down in the basements, as if the whole College were one tightly packed bundle, wires ignited in a multiple magnetic surge, apparently caused by the overcharged atmosphere, and began to flail about like living whips of fire, striking at the parquetry floors, the wall paneling, and the coffered ceilings. Like skilled gauchos, they lassoed armchairs and tables, slipped under the carpets and made them ripple, snapping at the bookshelves with their red-hot copper tips. Nothing flammable escaped contact with the black wires torn from their casings by the violence of the short circuit and animated by the violent metamorphosis of the fairy Electricity into the witch Spontaneous Combustion. It was a moonless midnight. All the lights had been switched off. Everyone was asleep. Unseen, in the dark, the erratic strokes of that hysterical scribbling set fire to everything. The darkness was divided into irregular hemispheres, with flashes of red against the persisting black. The lines became volumes, intangible and mobile, which started to race around, sliding over all the surfaces. The flames began to open doors. The smoke, wearing three-dimensional neck-laces of sparks, surged into corridors and stairways. A number of the spot fires joined up before the alarm woke the sleepers. The sound of the burning was growing louder, like a beating of elytra and tambourines, or a million chicks marking micro-seconds. Enrique woke up in his dormitory, along with the other First House boys; they were already shouting and run-ning around. He stumbled after them in a daze, without even managing to put on his slippers but knowing what was going on. Like all children he knew what a house fire was, although, in his short life, he had never experienced one. Of course it is one thing to know what a fire is, and another to find one actu-ally happening. The group was moving like a breath expelled toward the door at one end of the room, although no one had told them to go that way and not the other. As he was about to pass through, Enrique turned back and saw the explana-tion: a huge fireball wobbling on the threshold at the far end of the dormitory. That was when he woke up properly. When he started running again, he found that he had been left behind. In a few steps he had caught up with the rest but he broke away almost immediately. In that unplanned evacuation, the thou-sand boarders were simultaneously running farther into the building and out of it; the College was beginning to reveal its strange reversibilities. Sleep was still present within each stu-dent. Disorientation was scaling new spatiotemporal heights. The lack of light didn't help. Although the flames shone, the smoke was black, and images appeared disjointedly, on twisted, fleeting planes. Enrique found himself in one unfamiliar place after another; all he could do was keep moving, accelerating constantly. Running, running, faster and faster ...

Was it a magical helper that materialized before him? Speed in the form of a girl, reaching out to him with a trusting smile? Whatever it may have been, there it was, in an elevated position, on the first landing of a spiral staircase. It was Leticia. Not an apparition but a flesh-and-blood girl. And what had seemed at first to be calmness in the midst of disaster, a well-meaning smile, was in fact terror-stricken paralysis and an appeal for help.

Even setting the supernatural aside, Enrique was right to be astonished by the girl who was looking at him. Her silhouette stood out against a black background from which pink highlights emerged, advancing toward a foreground that was difficult to locate. Distant-seeming flashes filtered through the strands of her long blonde hair. The hand that she was holding out was white and small with very slim fingers, like the slender toes of her little bare feet below the hem of her nightgown. Something was telling Enrique that it wasn't the moment to wonder how she got there; what mattered was not being there, but getting out ... and yet the fact remained that she was a girl. And the College, as far as he was aware, was a boarding school for boys; that was how he had thought of the place in the months he had spent there, and he couldn't change his idea of it just like that. The presence of a girl from a girl's dormitory, who, like him, had escaped without having had time to get dressed, plunged him into the bafflement produced by doublings and parallel universes. He didn't know how far or in what direction he had traveled along those smoky corridors, but it was as if he had reached the "other side," where everything was back to front. And the strangest thing was that the same thoughts must have been occurring to her.

A huge hand threw fistfuls of yellow ash in his face. In three little jumps, light as a bug, Leticia came down to his level, and a moment later (the whole encounter lasted no more than a couple of seconds), Enrique had taken her by the hand and they were both running again.

Inexplicable and unexplained as it was, their meeting gave them a sense of security. They decided that wherever one of them went, the other would go too; that way they couldn't get lost. Because they weren't obeying instructions, it suddenly seemed like a game: they could advance or retreat, go up or down. They abandoned themselves to chance and movement; it was almost too easy. There was a sense of great freedom: a clarion call marking the quick and painless end of childhood. So simple or ineluctable did it seem, their escape from the burning College.

But none of the students they encountered, alone or in groups, seemed to have any idea which direction would lead to the exit (the sign that said "Direction" was no help because it referred to the Director's office). When one group came across another running the opposite way, they shouted questions, orders, and suggestions, which were met with flat refusals or doubts; but sometimes the two groups persuaded each other, and turned around and ran off in opposite directions once again, without waiting to see what the other group was doing. As in a nightmare, some saw children like themselves, running, hair and clothes on fire, and only when the mirrors exploded into drops of liquid silver did they realize that they had seen themselves reflected.

Running over the game like melting paint, anguish and panic were the two guiding threads; they got tangled in the bubbles of ignited oxygen, forming knots which exploded, flinging mutely screaming boys and girls through endless corridors and classrooms. Some were still wondering what was going on. There were still whole sectors of the College—rows of classrooms, assembly halls, offices—that were quivering in the dark, far from the fire. But the affected and unaffected areas were juxtaposed, and soon superposed. On the third story, something collapsed with a great crash: the floor of a dormitory gave way and fell through to the story below. The students had been asleep; they went flying in their beds, while the sheets, sucked into the void, flew up like fancy-dress ghosts. With their jutting corners of fire, the spaces pushed and morphed into one another. The many laboratories and workshops required by the College's approach to learning burst into flames in different ways, at different speeds, making the fire a multidimensional phenomenon. Like all the others, Leticia and Enrique were lost, wandering among specters of masonry, while pots of burning flowers went flying overhead: glittering bouquets that plunged into concave obscurities, where compact, foaming glows appeared. The children's pupils had shrunk down to pinpoints, so the zones of darkness seemed like tunnels suddenly full of voices. It was as if they were entering the successive, inmost hearts of the castle. The volume of the crackling had been increasing steadily, and now it was deafening. The legendary multitude of boarders, a thousand strong, circulated in this palace of applause like molecules programmed by a mad chemist. Whenever Enrique and Leticia, still hand in hand, came to one of the hollows opened by the fire, and the glow made it possible for them to see, they looked at each other's faces, as if to make sure that it was still them. With everything collapsing, the routes from A to B had become unrecognizable, although perhaps in their blind flight they had entered a sector of the building that was unknown to them. Did they really know any part of it? The sense of danger was mounting. They ran through a large assembly hall whose windows shattered one after another. Because of the pressure differential, the burning ceiling attracted gray cones of pulverized glass. A group of older students, from the senior classes, came bursting into the hall through the door that Enrique and Leticia had been running toward. The pair realized that they had been leading a sizeable contingent of fugitives; seniors and juniors jumbled together in a circuit of collisions that left sooty marks in space. By chance, the two came out onto a high gallery overlooking a covered patio: Botany's panoramic winter garden. The little trees in pots along the edge were shaking their rounded crowns as if possessed: the fire contained its own wind. From that elevated vantage point, Enrique and Leticia saw all the specimens of imprisoned flora bursting into flames: the calyces inflated with searing air generated globular explosions; wavy strings of incandescent alveoli rose up and floated before their eyes. Following the gallery around to the other side, they saw a stairway, but they also saw the fire that was climbing it. They went down a dark passageway off to the side. Pictures were falling noisily from the walls, and for a fluid instant, before they were burned to a cinder, the watercolors showed various views of the College's interior. The pair ran through a series of small rooms, all empty, which must have been the apartments where the teachers and caretakers lived. What had become of them? Could they have fled? It was as if they had never existed. Noticing their absence, Leticia and Enrique realized that the other students had disappeared too. They were alone. They sped up, in a surge of renewed panic, scared that they might have started running in circles. The College staff, whatever their qualifications, were treated as servants, and had to spend their scant hours of rest in this poky hive. The smallness of the rooms intensified the impression of a false labyrinth. The smoke was getting denser too, but just when it seemed impenetrable, there was a draught of fresh air, and they fell down a marble staircase, tumbling over each other at each turn of the tight spiral. By the time they reached the bottom, they could barely tell bottom from top, but they got to their feet and dashed off again, dodging the falling beams, running over a carpet of tiny and mercifully sparse flames. Now they really were at the heart of the conflagration. And they didn't see anyone else there. Had all the others managed to get out? Were they the last ones left? They seemed to be near an exit, to judge by the blasts of air shoving them this way and that. But those same blasts were fanning the flames, which were becoming gigantic and moving at lightning speed.

Then they witnessed a spectacle that imprinted itself on their retinas forever and formed a secret bond between them. An enormous suction cup wrenched open a hole in a wall, through which thirty or forty priests in cassocks came running like so many rats. They were running for their lives, and their desperation made the animal simile (rats, crows, dogs) perfectly apt. Some were young, others older, elderly even, but all were animated by the same mechanical, frenetic vitality. The will to save themselves had given them wings; in the emergency, earthly existence had become more important than the hope of salvation beyond the grave or recompense for martyrdom. They were shouting, but nothing could be heard over the continuous roar of the fire. The collapses and explosions did not stop them. Where they had to, they leaped over the flames, with a furious concentration, cassocks billowing. Within seconds they reached the place where Enrique and Leticia were standing, frozen by surprise, and went on past without even looking at them. The two children turned and saw them rushing into a vortex of black smoke. They were Jesuits. It had taken the outbreak of a fire to reveal their existence behind the mask of progressive, secular thought and German theosophy. Their passing had lasted the briefest moment; the two little fugitives followed them, guided by a reliable instinct, although, in that direction, the whirls of fire and black wind were growing more violent. And soon, in fact, Enrique and Leticia were falling. They plummeted, at staggering speed—and just in time—while the rest of the College was reduced to nothing. It was because of moths that the building had maintained its form up until the previous second. The trees in the grounds were home to an infinite number of their larvae. This inordinate quantity was a natural protective mechanism, very common among those species which are most exposed to predation. Each moth laid one or two million eggs in the expectation that birds would eat almost all of the larvae, but that, out of such a vast number, two or three would be bound to survive, or one in any case, which would be enough to fulfil the insect's reproductive mission. Before eating the larvae, the birds waited until they had attained a certain stage of development and were at their tastiest. The larvae had not yet reached that stage on the night of the fire, which was why the full contingent remained intact. And the heat hastened their maturation: they opened their wings all at once, in unprecedented numbers, and rushed toward the brightness of the flames, drawn by an irresistible atavism. They all flattened themselves against the burning building, suicidally: such tiny, barely individuated creatures pay no heed to death as long as they are obeying the instructions of instinct (as if they were thinking, "It knows best"). There were so many of them, so many thousands of millions, that the live (but dying) elastic layer covered every millimeter of the enormous castle, not just the walls and the roof, but every one of its cornices, and the front steps, the coats of arms and sculpted figures, even the shutters on the windows and the handles on the doors. The entire building was there, in every one of its details, but made of moths. This architectural simulacrum, which now really was the palace of dreams, a translucent edifice of dark moth wings, remained in place for a few seconds after the real building had fallen in, and then the great membrane burned all at once in a single blaze and disappeared. Precisely at that moment, Leticia and Enrique landed on the floor of the old billiard room in the basement, disused since the previous owners of the mansion had sold it to the Company. But there was still a table, with its threadbare green baize, and on it a scale model of the College, in which the thousand boarders had sought refuge. This extremely ingenious evacuation plan was based on the safeguards provided by a sudden change of dimensions. The two children hesitated. But they had no choice. All the others had gone in; they were the last. Glancing over their shoulders they saw the monster blaze descending upon them ...

They didn't see how they could possibly fit into the model, which was no bigger than a trunk, given that there were two of them (they had no intention of splitting up) nor how, once inside, they were supposed to run until they found the way out, not to mention the fact that a thousand others had already gone in ... But this second College was famous for reproducing every detail of the real College with the utmost precision, which guaranteed that there would be space.

And indeed, although it was tight, the two children did manage to squeeze in. The problem was that they couldn't see a thing. But a solution soon presented itself: the invisibly fine filaments that had been used to represent the wiring sprang loose and began to glow. It was as if they had been waiting for the last two to enter. The inside of the miniature began to shine like a lamp. Perhaps it had been designed as a "beacon of learning." Gaping in wonder, Enrique and Leticia contemplated the Lilliputian masterpiece, in which each room, each piece of furniture, each object was reproduced down to the minutest detail. So realistic was the effect that each thing seemed to be not a reproduction but the original itself, seen through a pane of glass. The time, patience, and skill that had been lavished on the model were now under threat. For the filaments, possessed of a violent electrical vitality, were beginning to transmit their light, in the form of fire, to everything they touched. They jumped, twisted and lassoed the armchairs as if thrown by dexterous cowboys; they wriggled in under the carpets and out the other side, rippling and slashing them with lines of flame, or cracked like whips against the shelves laden with books, which in spite of their tiny dimensions (0.1 by 0.18 millimeters) had pages covered in text. How hard they would have been to read! thought the children, for whom normal books were still a struggle. You would have to use a powerful microscope, sliding the words under the lens. The darkness was divided into tiny irregular hemispheres, marked with red dots that showed up against the enduring ground of black. Although the lines were minimal, with barely any length to speak of, they turned into mobile, intangible volumes, and began to race away, sliding over all the surfaces. The fire was beginning everywhere at once, the smoke springing up like gray mushrooms that repeated and transformed themselves, turning somersaults. But could there be such tiny mushrooms? Penicillin fungi, perhaps. The flames created their own circulation, opening toy doors that had been closed, and closing the doors that were open, which incidentally showed how well finished the model was: all the doors worked, and the locks had little shiny keys. Some spot fires, centimeters apart, joined up before the alarm was raised and the running and shouting began. There was a sound of extremely rapid ticking, so soft that it was inaudible in all but its highest frequencies. The flow of time must have been swifter in that dimension. Leticia and Enrique had not expected to find a fire in the model as well; there had been no time to expect anything, but unconsciously they had supposed that there would be some respite. They were disheartened to find that the effort and discomfort of submitting to the shrinkage had been futile. But it was even more futile to complain, so they ran for their lives down the corridors of the College in flames, although this time it was the Mini-College So small were the distances, a step sufficed to cover them, almost before it had been taken. But this advantage turned out to be worthless, since it was granted to the fire as well. Although they had never experienced a fire in a space scaled down by a factor of a hundred, they could deduce how it worked. How difficult could it be to get out of a "building" that was smaller than they were? They maintained their conviction that it "wasn't real." Those little beds made of toothpicks, with their perfectly imitated tissue-paper sheets, complete with hems, exploding tinily into flames and curling up like snails as they burned, the children could have blown them out with a breath. To say so might have calmed them down. But when they tried to speak, particles of smoke got caught in their throats and made them cough. Their coughing shook the walls and the roof, and created indoor cyclones that intensified the flames. Sooner than they would have liked, Leticia and Enrique found themselves running with the same thousand students, all bumping into each other in an unimaginable crush. In the midst of this chaos, two contradictory reactions prevailed: the thought that a fire in miniature could have no serious consequences, and fear of the same fire, which since it had no reference magnitude could turn out to be fatal on any scale. The lack of light didn't help. Although the glow of the little flames was intense, the moving bodies of so many children, huge by comparison, threw shadows in every direction; images appeared disjointedly on twisted, fleeting planes. The urgency was intensifying, not only because the reduced dimensions made everything more immediate (salvation and ruin were staring them right in the face), but also because this episode was a "second chance," like a supplementary test, and there would be no third.

Although everything was supposed to be the same, some things had changed in the reduction. Fire, for example, whose consistency and texture had undergone an alteration: it was brighter and more compact, and went rolling through the air with a liquid agility, like quicksilver. It gave the impression that its effect would be to prick rather than burn. But they didn't wait around to find out.

They ran through a girls' dormitory. Enrique saw for himself that there was an unknown reverse to the obverse that was the dormitory for boys. The central hallway running from one end to the other was no more than a foot long; the real girls in their miniature beds seemed enormous, like bears wedged into thimbles. They screamed in sham terror, competing to see who could make the most noise, but when blue sheets of flame enveloped them, the game became real; they leaped and fled. Several followed Leticia and Enrique, but before they reached the stairs, which would have been a squeeze for a little toy soldier, the group was dispersed into various dark hallways by a crowd heading in the opposite direction. Masses of students were crammed into other, still narrower stairways, testing each other's temperature with tentative fingers until they got burned, then taking fright and thrashing around crazily to free themselves from the pent-up knot of bodies. Everyone was subject to the same psychological mechanism that Leticia and Enrique had observed in themselves: at first it was fun, a game, this model in which reality wasn't true; then came fear, as they realized that, true or not, reality was prevailing. In the collision of disparate dimensions, the instinct for survival may have been neutralized or thrown into confusion. No one dared ask if anyone else still had the desire or the need to get out, because they suspected that the answer would be "No," and that was a truth they preferred not to face. The only thing they knew for sure was that they couldn't expect any help; on the contrary, they had to expect that the senseless, mechanical actions of the others would disorient and obstruct them. But come to think of it, they hadn't received any help in the previous sequence either, except for the favors of chance. Whole sectors of the palace, occupying the space of a grain of rice, rows of classrooms, assembly halls, offices, and various other monuments to the skill of the miniature model maker, remained peaceful and quiet, untouched by the fire. But the affected and unaffected areas were contiguous, more so than ever, and since the fire was matter's response to contiguity, the conflagration was already everywhere. A crash was heard from the third story, sounding now like the "tock" of a chopstick on a rice bowl: the floor of a dormitory had collapsed, and the children who slept there, while wriggling to maintain their balance on the tiny beds, absurdly covered with sheets that were barely more than a single thread, pretended to go on sleeping as, beds and all, they fell down to the story below. This microcatastrophe within the microcatastrophe was an indication that contiguity had intensified to the point where its nature was beginning to change. The spaces, so tiny it was hard to see how anything could fit into them, seemed to want to show that they could in fact hold something, after all: space. With their jutting wings of fire, they pushed and morphed into one another. The many laboratories and workshops, reproduced with breathtaking exactitude (each test tube a single sparkle of glass), exploded in different ways, at different speeds, making the fire a multidimensional phenomenon. Feeling more like intruders than ever, Leticia and Enrique wandered among ghosts of woodwork, canvases and chemistry flasks, a wandering that required them to shift their bodies no more than a millimeter: they saw pots of burning flowers fly past over their heads, glittering bouquets that plunged into concave obscurities, where compact, foaming glows appeared. And all this was happening in the palm of one hand; it took an effort of concentration to imagine the fire life-size, which was the only way to understand or at least conceive of it. But the children had no time for mental exercises, which would have been a rash indulgence in the circumstances. They had to keep fleeing, although the zones of light and darkness all seemed as fine as hairs. They were entering the successive, inmost hearts of the model. When Leticia and Enrique, still hand in hand, faces large as lecture theatres, paused in front of one of the hollows opened by the fire, which were as tiny as pinholes, they glimpsed lateral vistas of destruction. Where some of the cardboard and papier-mâché that represented the walls had collapsed, the routes from A to B had become unrecognizable (if it makes any sense to call those immediate proximities routes), although, given the limited space that the College was now occupying, with meters converted to centimeters, perhaps a mere doubting tilt of their heads had revealed a part of the building that was unknown to them. With their eyes if not their feet, they traversed a large assembly hall whose windows shattered one after another: the craftsman's expertise had created a "life-size" impression, and the windows, with their panes cut from greaseproof paper, reproduced the shatterings with subatomic puffs of ash. Soon Leticia and Enrique found themselves in the high gallery that gave onto the big assembly hall, big in relative terms of course, because now it must have measured five centimeters from wall to wall. The fire was there already. Red grids of flame were spreading over the coffered ceiling, shedding tears of gray smoke, which floated in midair. The sparks, traditional conveyors of fire, already small in themselves, were scaled down to veritable points in this model. Fire filled the piano, which exploded, throwing out a chrysanthemum of mahogany and ivory fragments, hammers and keys, in all directions. It was sad to see a miniature that must have required hundreds, perhaps thousands of hours of work with the finest tweezers and microscopes destroyed like that, in an instant. What creature from the realm of almost nothing, with fingers a thousand times finer than a spider's leg, could have played Chopin's *Nocturnes* on that piano? The same thing was happening to all the contents of that magical doll's house, but the piano, a supreme feat of precision bricolage, made a stronger impression. As if possessed, the little trees in pots along the walls were shaking their rounded crowns, each composed of a single cell in karyokinesis. On the other side of the hall there was a stairway leading up to the opposite gallery, but fire was climbing it, in the form of little flames cut from blue glazed paper. The pictures, reproduced with the same exactitude as the rest, fell from the walls with drop-like "plocks." There was something that didn't quite add up, because common sense suggested that fire could not be reduced in scale in the same way as a concrete object. And if it went on being the same, this posed a problem, one of the many to be solved according to the "simple rule of three" that governed the passage from one set of dimensions to the other. If the College had burned down in five minutes, how long would it take for the blaze to consume its reproduction at a scale of one to a hundred? If fire was irreducible, there must have been a reduction of time itself. Perhaps this was normal in cases of traumatic repetition. The gallery was so narrow that it ran in one direction only, and led to a labyrinth of little dormitories. With what they charged for tuition and board, it was scandalous that the self-proclaimed progressive, liberal owners of the College had given their teaching staff, who were already underpaid, rooms so poky and stuffy that a dwarf, correction: a Playmobil figure, would have had to bend double or quadruple to squeeze in. The doll's house dimensions of those cubicles reinforced the persistent impression that a single stamp of the foot would have been enough to put out the fire. But this might just have been a ploy to make the children lower their guard. They hurried, but jammed as they were in the general crush, they could barely swivel their eyeballs. They tried to push through to a space where they would have a choice of doors, rather than being obliged to go through the one in front of them. The walls of the rooms began to sweat fire. Starting to panic, Enrique and Leticia feared that their gaze was running around in circles, although it was hard to see how there could be circles in a place where straight lines barely had room to move. As the smoke grew thicker, they had to feel their way forward, but suddenly a concentrated gust of cold air forced them down. It was amazing that a blast as fine as a needle could exert such force, but plausible given the rules of the game that they now seemed to be playing. In any case, they were falling, head over heels, down a spiral staircase made of tiny pieces of marble cut by an underworld jeweler, which even imitated the sagging curves of long-worn steps in public buildings. The tumble was of some use, since it wasn't so crowded down at the bottom: there was a little space, several centimeters wide, between them and a wall. They had no choice but to look at this wall: their heads were locked into place, temple to temple. And held there, as in a microscopic cinema, they saw the repetition of a spectacle that imprinted itself on their retinas forever and formed a secret bond between them. A suction cup the size of a speck of dust wrenched open a hole in the wall, and several thousand priests in cassocks came running out. They were Jesuits, the Jesuits who had always been pulling the strings behind the College's facade of secularism and innovative pedagogy. The increase in numbers was due to the fact that each priest consisted of a single atom. But even under this maximal compression they retained their characteristics: some were young, others older, even elderly, from the time when Ignacio de Loyola had founded the order, but being atoms gave them a prodigious agility. The collapses and explosions did not stop them; they could even slip between the atoms of the plaster. There was no room for pretense between their protons and electrons, and they all fled from death at the speed of light, each for himself, with the egoism of matter, confirming, had there been any doubt, that there is no other world than this.

LETICIA LOOKED AT HIM AND SMILED. DEEPLY MOVED, Enrique held the gaze of his long-lost friend. But then, with a sigh, he looked away, and there was another surprise. As before, there was no need to turn around or change his posture; he was still in the place where the water had doused him—it was still flowing over his body—and he was holding the handlebar of his bike with his left hand. His pupils swiveled just enough for his gaze to shift from Leticia's face to mine. He raised his eyebrows in astonishment, which altered the flow of the water over his face, diverting it around his shallow eye sockets.

"Kent!"

Hearing my name, I was momentarily baffled. Had I misheard? Did he mean me? All of a sudden, I had to recover the self-consciousness of which I had been stripped by the earlier surprise. But it took only a moment, barely that. I opened my arms, rose to my feet smiling broadly, and went over to him:

"Enrique!"

I knew him, I knew him very well, although I hadn't known him long: he was the owner of the guest house where I was staying. Why hadn't I recognized him before? I didn't have Leticia's excuse; she hadn't seen him for years. I had seen him that very morning, and the previous evening we had talked for hours. And yet there was an explanation: I hadn't noticed him before he was doused by that gush of water, and that was what I saw: the gush, the accident, and then, straight away, the encounter with Leticia, their mutual recognition; and her "Enrique!" had been so charged with personal memories that I had failed to make the connection with the "Enrique" I knew, the owner of the guest house.

IT WAS A CASUAL BUT HIGH-END GUEST HOUSE, CATER-
ing to a cosmopolitan, educated clientele, who were very fussy
in certain respects and not at all in others, according to the dic-
tates of fashion. It had opened at a time when "thematic" hotels and guest houses were springing up everywhere: the decor,
the staff, the service, the general atmosphere, everything had
to be related to a particular theme, be it Buddhism, Polar Ex-
ploration, Classical Music, the Middle Ages, Under the Sea,
Tango, Film Noir, or thousands of others. As Buenos Aires became a Mecca for tourists, these establishments multiplied to
the point where it was hard to find a theme that hadn't been
used. The choice itself, which required no more than a little
imagination or, failing that, a dictionary to open at random,
was only the first step. Then it was a matter of exercising a certain artistic or theatrical flair, in order to ensure that the place
fulfilled the promise of its founding concept. The realizations
varied in thoroughness and quality. Some people simply went
through the motions, without really committing to the idea:
they looked for something easy, like Polynesia, put up some
posters of surfers and reproductions of Gauguin, and that was
it. Others went overboard: every last coffee spoon had to be
somehow related to the theme, which created an oppressive

atmosphere; it was like a relentless, inescapable masquerade. With the influx of visitors, establishments with morbid, even disgusting themes began to appear (Death Metal, Hospital, Twisted Crime), proving that there is a public for everything. Partly because the obvious (and less obvious) options were already "occupied," and partly because of the progression or emulation that fashions always generate, some entrepreneurs chose odd and provocative concepts, which were difficult to illustrate, like the Complement. My young friend faced none of these problems; he didn't fall into any of these traps, because his choice had been settled from the start, and it turned out to be very apt and productive: Evolution. This was not an arbitrary choice like those of his colleagues; it wasn't prompted by the desire to surprise or find an easy option or set himself the challenge of matching the ambience to the theme. It was, in his case, a deep-rooted predilection, a former passion, and because of this long affinity it was natural for him to expand on the theme and live with it. And the exercise went beyond simple illustration; it took on new dimensions, since the concept of Evolution, as well as being illustrated on the walls and in the furniture, could be made manifest or actualized in the life of the guest house as a commercial enterprise: it evolved as the client base grew and technological innovations were adopted, as glitches were ironed out and the service was continually improved. Within the first few days of my stay I had noticed this evolutionary movement, not as movement naturally, but as a climate, a disposition to impermanence and change, which

adapted itself (in good evolutionary fashion) to the mental climate of travel.

Enrique's intellectual commitment to Evolution was the
gratefully cherished remnant of a former enthusiasm: one of
those all-consuming passions so typical of youth. At the age of
twenty, on a friend's recommendation, he had read Darwin's
masterwork. He was immediately dazzled, and this initial excitement was only affirmed and intensified by sharing his wonder with the friend who had recommended the book, and then
with others to whom they recommended it in turn. In those
pages they found all the answers, even to questions that they had
thought could never be formulated. Seen through that magic
lens, the world was clarified. Those young minds ascended to
ecstatic levels as they perceived the mechanisms that made the
world a world and beings beings. Darwinism, for them, was like
a diamond of supreme beauty turning at the center of the natural sphere. Only those who have experienced it can understand
the elation that this knowledge brings. Partly as a joke, but partly
in earnest too, they founded the Evolution Club, and organized
discussions, visits to the Natural History Museum, and excursions to green spaces in the environs of Buenos Aires. It lasted
a year or a little more. Such passions are never long-lived. The
members gradually drifted apart, yielding to the demands of
study and work that are so pressing in early adulthood, and their
Darwinist convictions, while never rejected, began to recede.
Ten years later, had they been asked to specify the peerless merit
of the discovery made by the sage of Downe, they would have

been at a loss. Or perhaps not, but they would have had to go haltingly, almost blindly, back into the labyrinth of discursive logic, and wander there until they reached that center—the diamond—where they had been so happy. As it happened nobody asked, or not insistently enough, so they were content to look back from a distance. They didn't regret that phase of their lives, or having lived it so intensely. At most, they might have wondered if they hadn't gone slightly overboard. They couldn't reconstruct the reasoning that they had used to generalize the theory's explanatory power. They clearly remembered having done this, but not how. Evolution (or was it adaptation? whatever, it was the same in the end) supplied the reasons why birds sang, and plane trees lost their leaves in autumn, but also why clocks had two hands, and some people stuttered, and Jupiter was bigger than Saturn. It was the universal key, putting time to work on behalf of thought. And in their ardor to understand, the members of the club were seized by vertigo. Hadn't it even occurred to them that the whole world might be one giant Evolution Club, within which theirs was a scale model, a cell? When the ardor died away and the club broke up, their lives went on. Not that they had been standing still; on the contrary, it had been an accelerated phase, after which a normal rhythm was resumed. Perhaps they felt that Evolution had acted on them too. How could it have been otherwise? It was acting still, and would never stop, and all the changes and adventures that lay in store for them would unfold according to its laws.

The life of the club was short, as I said: a year, more or less.

And it was only during the first month, or three weeks, that Evolution was the primary focus. Almost from the start, in fact, the attention of the members was diverted by the arrival of a newcomer who had no interest in the subject. The informal manner in which the young enthusiasts ran their meetings made it possible for Jusepe, who was already friends with a number of them, to join their group without having been drawn to it by Darwinism. He turned the talk toward his own interests, which at first seemed worthy of attention, because the young man was a sculptor. Before long, there was no more talk of Evolution at the meetings. Or of sculpture. Although Jusepe claimed to be a skilled practitioner of the art (he never supplied any proof of this), he had neither the narrative skill required to tell his story, nor the conceptual capacity to reason or theorize. It was odd and almost inexplicable that in spite of these limitations, he was able to dominate the rest single-handedly, especially considering the passion that had brought the others together. Jusepe's triumph was not deliberate, far from it. It was largely due to the force of his personality, an attraction or magnetism that was simply a part of his nature. He dominated by virtue of his mere animal presence; no more was required. Not that he had much more to offer: neither education, nor charm, nor any real talent. But dominate he did, becoming the center of that little group of friends, and since he had no interest in Evolution, the subject was never raised again. The grounds of his authority, which he exercised unwittingly and never set out to secure, are to be sought not only in his assertiveness, but also in the contrast between him and the other members of the club. He came from the humblest of backgrounds, while they were the scions of wealthy, cultivated families (their parents were businesspeople, lawyers, psychoanalysts). Not that he insisted on his origins. He didn't have to; it was obvious from his nonchalant roughness, his unrefined manners, and the way he kept spitting on the floor. He was also a talker; wherever he was, no one else could get a word in. He spoke with the monotonous intonation of those who haven't had the chance to learn that sentences are composed of subjects and predicates. His themes were basic: football, women, money. Since he didn't read the papers, he had little new to say about those working-class staples, but he said it interminably, brooking no interruptions. He complained about the millions that football players were paid; women he hated with a vengeance, no doubt because he suspected that no woman would ever look at him twice (he was very ugly); as to money, either he bragged about how much he was going to earn in the future, or he complained about how the rich and the corrupt were keeping it all for themselves. He always seemed indignant, but it was the resigned indignation of the downtrodden, the ancestral victims of history. He made the others feel guilty about their privileges; they were paralyzed by a kind of appalled fascination. Although they never admitted it to each other or themselves, they were ashamed of having done something as useless, from the point of view of Jusepe's brute reality, as reading Darwin and believing in Evolution. They simply never mentioned it again.

And yet, by virtue of the spell that they themselves had created, Evolution remained present, if only as a metaphor. As in a magician's trick—"the hand is swifter than the eye"—Jusepe had replaced Evolution; where one had been, the other was now, but the substitution was not complete; a kind of conceptual ghost was left floating, which manifested itself in the story of the young sculptor.

His family background cannot have been all that crucial in the formation of his character, because his parents got rid of him before he was ten by apprenticing him to a sculptor. It was a rather barbaric decision, a hangover from a bygone age, when people were less concerned with the psychological development and legal rights of children. In a different milieu the parents might have been prosecuted because they simply abandoned Jusepe (indeed he never saw them again). And there was an aggravating circumstance: they didn't even know the man to whom they entrusted their son. Someone had told them that a sculptor who lived in his studio was looking for a young helper to replace the previous boy, who had died. That precedent and the prospects it suggested were hair-raising, but Jusepe's parents didn't care. Unwittingly, they were submitting one of medieval Europe's most productive institutions—apprenticeship—to a totally anachronistic test. In its place and time, that tradition had preserved knowledge and skills by handing them down in a vital and practical way. But those virtues could be turned around, and their effects, intensified by the inversion, could prove fatal. In Jusepe's case, they were fatal to his soul, which led in turn to the definitive loss of all manners. The apprenticeship should have had the opposite effect. Daily contact with an artist should have refined his behavior. But the conditions in which that contact occurred made him obtuse and brutal. If any civilized traits had remained from the years of early childhood that he had spent with his family, they disappeared in the company of Mandam. It could not have been otherwise, for the sculptor was a genuine savage. Already unruly by nature, he had found an excuse in art, or a corrupted myth of the artist, to indulge his lowest urges without any kind of restraint. He was able to get away with it because of the reclusive life he led, in a shed at the end of the strip of slums in Quilmes, where the garbage dumps and vacant lots along the river are home to a shifting population of vagrants and criminals. He never went out (which is why he needed an "errand boy") or talked to anyone. It was only by some kind of negative miracle that Jusepe's parents had learned of his existence. The boy's life was plunged into darkness, metaphorically but literally too, because the shed that was now his dwelling had no windows, and the roller door that had served as an entrance when the place had been used for storage was broken and could no longer be raised. They went in and out through an opening in the side: not a door but a hole that they covered with planks. There was one camp bed, and the old man slept on it almost all day, in that dark space populated by rats and monstrous forms, while the boy lay curled up in the corner, hearing Mandam snore, and nursing an anguish so constant that he eventually ceased to feel

it. He didn't dare wander around outside, not only because the
sculptor had forbidden him to, but also because he was scared
of the stray dogs that bred in those forsaken marshes. Mandam
would wake up in the afternoon and, in the wild dementia of
his hangovers, throw himself into frenetic pseudoactivity. First,
he would give the boy a hiding, then he would send him to
the shop to buy food and wine. At that point, Jusepe had no
choice: he had to face the dogs. His fear was reasonable: those
animals had histories of bloody violence, which had failed to
achieve notoriety only because no one had bothered to bring
them to the attention of the public. It was a euphemism to say
that Mandam sent Jusepe to buy provisions: his orders were to
ask for credit, or, failing that, to beg or steal. He would be re-
warded with another beating. And that was not the end of his
labors and sorrows; they had barely begun. The humiliation
of begging, and not even for himself, with the added trauma
of the dogs, was nothing compared to what awaited him in the
shed as the night wore on and intoxication kindled his master's
delusions of industry. Then the shifting began: the big rocks
that formed a mountain in the dark depths of the shed had to
be moved from one place to another. Jusepe, weak, malnour-
ished, starving, a bundle of sleepless, fearful nerves, executed
orders that were increasingly hard to understand as Mandam
began to slur his words. In fact, the old man didn't know what
he wanted. He wanted a fifty-kilo rock that was right at the back
to be placed in the middle of the shed so that he could see it
better. But being able to see it better turned out to be no use to

him. He wanted to see it side by side with another rock that he had previously told Jusepe to put down the back. Or he would take it into his head to stand the rocks on their most convex surfaces, making them wobble uncontrollably so that others had to be dragged over to prop them up. The light of the candle stub didn't reach into the corners of the shed, and Jusepe had to feel his way forward, tripping as he went, and flushing out rats and spiders that were no less frightening for being invisible—on the contrary. How had those rocks got there in the first place? It was a mystery, like their composition. They weren't marble or granite. They must have been some kind of limestone. Irregularly shaped, they had hollows and protuberances, which were occasionally crushed in the shifting, producing a dust that shone in the darkness when the candle eventually went out. It was also something of a mystery why an individual who did nothing with rocks but have them shifted from place to place had gone on considering himself a sculptor. Had Mandam practiced sculpture at some point in his life? There was nothing there in the shed to prove that he had. But this mystery could be explained by the abuse of cheap alcohol and the softening of his brain. And in any case, it was interesting as a lesson: people can sincerely believe that they are something they are not, and even govern their lives according to that belief. The lesson was of limited use, however, since it indicated only what not to do. Jusepe learned more, in a piecemeal way, from the life that he found himself forced to lead in those years. He matured more quickly than he would have in a normal environment. And if, in the process, he became more brutal, that was neither here nor there. Survival is survival, after all, and it is the same for rich and poor, for the barbaric and the civilized.

One of Jusepe's first independent acts had to do with the dogs, logically enough, since fear of them had initially confined him to the shed. Then he had been obliged to face them in those gloomy dusks, as he made his way to Don Inocencio's store. The dogs roamed in large packs and were all the same: long-limbed, skinny, short-coated animals, with eyes on the sides of their heads, almost like the eyes of horses, except that their gaze was human and bad: anxious, full of hate and fear. It was as if those eyes were not theirs. Knowing that the dogs were especially partial to the aborted fetuses and babies dumped in that zone by people from the shantytowns along the shore, Jusepe made the connection, and from then on he was convinced of the humanity in their gaze, a humanity that sprang from the other side of the human. Apart from scaring him, the dogs left him alone. At first he thought they hadn't noticed him, but after a while he began to feel that they were afraid of him for some reason. Perhaps it was his smell, or something else about him that only they could discern. Sometimes, when darkness had fallen, he could see a white halo shining around his hands, his legs, his feet and even his footprints: this, he presumed, was a result of contact with Mandam's rocks, and he suspected that the shimmer was what kept the dogs away. He might also have considered the possibility that they were ignoring him because they were busy with their own affairs. As indeed they were.

They were constantly having sex. The males lined up behind the females on heat, but the succession was far from orderly because some dog was always getting stuck, and the pair would fall over and thrash about, kicking with its eight legs, snapping and biting with its two heads to fend off the waiting dogs who would fly into a rage and attack them. Sometimes, when this kind of spasm occurred, the stronger of the attached animals, the female as often as the male, would stand up and run away dragging the other one, which flailed about like a rag, twisting and kicking at the air, unable to get free, in the midst of fierce barking and attacks from the rest of the pack, by this stage more frenzied than ever. Even without these sexual accidents, violence would often break out. It was latent, a millimeter under the surface, and the slightest provocation could set it off: competition for a rat or a dug-up bone, or simply the need to vent the resentment they felt as pariahs, unloved and rejected by all. They were not strangers to cannibalism. The pups did not survive. The dogs didn't seem to care about the preservation of the species. And yet there were more and more of them. In the years that Jusepe spent in the shed, he saw their population grow. Sometimes they would disappear for days on end, and then the whole pack would return, following the carts drawn by skinny horses, and they would take up residence again along the shore, to reproduce frantically, and brawl, and bark all day and night in ceaseless rage. Jusepe noticed that in the midst of the chaos they created, there was always one curled up on the ground, sleeping peacefully, as if in another dimension. The frequent floods threw them into a panic. Their fights to the death with seagulls intensified, along with massacres of other birds, which left feathers scattered everywhere. Even so, it was hard to see how they could find enough to eat. They were thin, but athletic and nimble, not skeletal like the carters' horses that came and went along the shore. And a great many calories must have been required to fuel all that activity. Although this puzzle didn't keep Jusepe awake at night—he had his own nutritional problems—the pieces required to solve it were all there at his disposal. He had noticed that whenever one of the ships went past sounding its horn, on its way to unload at the Ensenada docks, the dogs ran to the water's edge and stood there watching it go by, still and quiet, some clearly tempted to dive in but too scared, as if they were adoring a munificent god. What kind of god or divinity could inspire reverence in those forsaken, dispossessed creatures? Only a distant god with smokestacks.

One day Jusepe witnessed a scene that should have shaken up all his ideas. It took place at Don Inocencio's store, where the boy went each afternoon. He heard the owner telling a client that he would be keeping it open later than usual because he was waiting for the vet, who was coming at his request to have a look at one of the dogs. Jusepe stayed to see what was going on. Curiosity overcame his fear of being punished for having delayed. When the vet, a young man in a white cotton scrub jacket, arrived with his pretty redheaded assistant, Don Inocencio explained that one of the females was looking unwell, coughing and spitting. He went to the door and called out: Daisy! Daisy! Come! An animal of average size came over and let herself be handled. The vet used his stethoscope, then examined the dog's mouth and eyes (with an ophthalmoscope) and, after consulting his assistant and listening when Daisy conveniently coughed, arrived at a diagnosis. He asked for a table on which to put the animal. Don Inocencio cleared a section of the counter. They placed the dog there, with her legs in the air. She didn't struggle, as if she knew that it was for her own good. The vet put on rubber gloves; the assistant took some instruments from a bag and moved to the other side of the counter, where she held the dog's head and, when the moment came, kept her mouth open. The vet shone a small flashlight down her throat and, using a long pair of silvery surgical tongs with curved tips, in a single movement, extracted a bone, which he displayed triumphantly. It was a fish bone: very fine and flexible, and only three centimeters long. It was hard to believe that something so insubstantial had caused so much discomfort to such a big animal, but as the vet explained, it had lodged itself in a very sensitive part of the body: a striated muscle. Relieved and happy, the dog jumped down off the counter and ran out to join the pack.

This event should have led Jusepe to question his presumptions about the dogs, and the state of neglect and general indifference in which, supposedly, they lived. He had always thought that no one looked after them, or cared whether they lived or died, but now he had discovered that an indisposition on the part of one of them could trigger a rescue operation ...

At the time he failed to grasp the lesson, but a seed had been planted.

With the inexorable flow of time, the boy was soon a boy no longer. As he had stopped being afraid of the dogs, he soon overcame his fear of the ghosts that had pursued him, and of his Master, who in the meantime had rapidly declined into old age and decrepitude. Neglected and ill-treated, Jusepe had to leap straight from childhood to the full autonomy of adult life. He missed out on the transitional phase, and with it all possibility of refining his manners. This is what happens when a person goes from the animal egoism of the child to the adult's prosaic practicality without the interlude of adolescence and its idealistic dreams. His role models were the derelicts and thieves with whom he began to associate. Various odd jobs of dubious legality gave him a measure of independence, and he started spending less time at the shed that had been his home. It was a natural progression from those jobs to small-time drug dealing, and he decided to style himself an artist (a "sculptor," since he had no knowledge of any other art), which gave him access to wealthy circles where he could sell his merchandise. The shed was an ideal place to stash his gear and hide out, but the real reason why he stayed there for longer than he needed to was that the dust from the rocks turned out to be ideal for cutting cocaine: it made his product phosphorescent, which boosted demand. Even so, he would have moved out earlier and found somewhere more comfortable, if not for an event that piqued his curiosity.

Mandam was already more or less bedridden, in the final stages of delirium tremens, and his acute arthritis made every movement painful and jerky. Nevertheless, his errand boy's absences had forced him to go out more often than before. It must have been those outings that reminded people of his existence, and some residents of Quilmes, moved by compassion perhaps at seeing him in such a bad way, took steps on his behalf. These resulted in a commission, the first that Jusepe had heard of, perhaps the first in the sculptor's whole life (although, having come so late, it was almost posthumous). The municipal Secretary of Culture came to the studio-shed in person to make a formal offer. They wanted a statue to upgrade the tree-lined square, which was getting a makeover. They gave Mandam free rein; it wasn't meant to be a commemorative monument but a purely aesthetic venture, something to inspire and raise the spirits of the local residents which, it has to be said, were in need of some elevation. The municipality didn't want to meddle in Mandam's choice of a theme, but it was suggested in the most tentative way that an allegory of Benevolence might be appropriate. No matter what he ended up choosing to do, there would be a plaque mentioning the distinguished artist who had honored the district by living and working there all his life. That life, it was plain to see, was only hours away from its term. Mandam had put on his best clothes for the occasion, replacing his usual holey T-shirt, pajama trousers, and flip-flops with a black frock coat, a cravat, gaiters, and a broad-brimmed hat: the anachronistic attire of a romantic artist, all of it moth-eaten and covered with dust. The Secretary was not surprised by this get-up, nor by the pigsty of a shed: it suited the image of the bohemian indifferent to material possessions. Jusepe, introduced by the old man as his assistant, witnessed the meeting with astonishment and, intrigued by the turn of events, stayed on at the shed for an extra day, although he had already decided to leave (he had rented an apartment on the corner of Güemes and Gallo). Only then did he realize how eager he was to see the sculptor at work, to find out how Mandam would go about it, and what the result would be: this curiosity had been building up in him for years. It grew so intense that he offered to drag an extra-big rock to the middle of the shed, as in the old days. In a state of overexcitement, the old man jigged about, muttering incoherently. He wasn't even able to get out of the outfit that he had donned to meet the Secretary of Culture and put on the work clothes that he didn't have, because he had never worked. He staggered around the rock in his usual way, except that in the past he had generally given up after a few minutes and flopped down on the camp bed with a glass of wine. This time, however, he persisted, talking to himself and grimacing. He even forgot to drink; it was true that he had almost stopped drinking by this stage; a single gulp was enough to bring his gravely debilitated system to the point of saturation, if it wasn't there already. He raised his hands in the direction of the rock and traced the outlines of what must have been the work he was hallucinating; he made frequent excursions to the corners of the shed, where he rummaged at random through piles of garbage without finding anything, only to rush back to the rock, even more bent over than before and moving with greater difficulty, constantly on the point of falling but held up by an inner force (art?) that had made an alliance with death and could therefore negotiate its abeyance. Hours went by. The sun set, and the dim light that came in through the opening in the wall of the shed faded and died. The coming and going continued in the dark. Jusepe, who all this time had been sitting on the ground with his back against the wall watching the old man's performance, lit a candle. By its light, Mandam's movements became more spectral. The boy observed the shadows thrown by his broad-brimmed hat, the knot of his cravat, the tails of his frock coat, and most of all by his hands, whose wild gestures projected monstrous and fleeting silhouettes of animals, planes, clouds and flowers onto the walls and the roof of the shed. Jusepe took the candle, which he had set on an empty box, and put it on the ground, closer to the center of the shed, which made the shadows larger and clearer; after a while, he moved it again, and then a few more times, adjusting and sharpening the fretwork of shadows. This was Jusepe's sole work of art: a private, secret work. The game was not purely visual; a soundtrack was provided by the old man's muttering, which gradually turned into hoarse and muted shouting. And there was a progression, but it took Jusepe some time to notice it. The pantomime was not entirely abstract: it represented the old sculptor's frustration at not being able to imprint his will upon the stone and give it a form. Once this had been understood, which wasn't easy, Mandam's movements made sense, and some of the words that he was muttering became comprehensible. He was looking for the tools he didn't have, the hammers, the chisels, the diamond tip, the polisher, and wondering where he had left them, who had moved them, imagining that thieves had broken in.... He was hallucinating. The tools, if he had ever possessed them, had been lost many decades ago, in a phase of his life so remote it might have belonged to another life entirely, completely divorced from his current existence. Suddenly his legs gave way, and he fell to his knees in front of the rock. He tried to raise his voice, which had diminished to an inaudible whisper, and shout at the mass rearing insensibly before him like a rustic idol, in no way resembling an allegory of Benevolence. Because of the flickering candle flame, the surface of the rock seemed to be rippling, and the shadows of the old man's fingers (his hands were raised in supplication) dipped intermittently into those ripples. As the flame wavered in the drafts, the twisted black hooks of his shadow-fingers grasped ineffectually at the stone. The old man fell silent, his mouth frozen in a twisted grimace. He was having an attack. He was seized by a convulsion, but he remained kneeling. In that ultimate moment, he opened his eyes wide and stared at Jusepe. And the young man, faced with this mute entreaty, was visited by inspiration. He put his hand into his pocket and pulled out a matchbox. He opened it. There was nothing inside, except for an almost invisible object. The candle had burned right down; its moribund, shrunken flame was dancing wildly, throwing the figures and shadows into a furious commotion. But this didn't prevent the old man from fixing his gaze on the hand, on the index finger and thumb emerging from the matchbox holding the bone that, years before, Jusepe had watched the vet remove from the throat of a dog. He had kept it as a souvenir, or amulet. He raised it and showed it to the old man. The slender spike of cartilage caught the last gleams of light. Although already seized by paralysis, Mandam reached out toward the magical object, in which he saw, at last, the tool with which to bore into the stone and give it all the forms of beauty. But Jusepe, having held the bone up for a moment to make sure that the old man had seen it clearly, replaced it unhurriedly in the box, put the box back in his pocket, pocketed his other hand and, whistling a hit song, in the dark now since the candle had finally died, walked out of the shed never to return.

Having consummated his revenge on the sculptor, Jusepe made his triumphal entry into life. But there was, and always would be, a residue. Neither his later membership of the Evolution Club nor his career in the world of crime were enough to heal the psychic wound inflicted by an episode from his childhood. In the end, he came to terms with everything else (a brutal father, a victimized mother, poverty, ignorance); after all, back then in Banfield it was not unusual for children to be subjected to the relentless violence of adults. Many, most, came through unscathed. The episode that scarred Jusepe so deeply, the narrative cocoon in which his father's verdict would lie forever coiled ("the kid's an idiot, a mental retard, a no-hoper"), was something like a divine judgment.

It happened one Sunday. Or on many Sundays ... Memory is generous in its cruelty. But it can't have been every Sunday because there was a roster, which was respected and argued over, since the duty in question was one that all the incumbents hated and tried to wriggle out of and only discharged, reluctantly, when it was their turn beyond any shadow of doubt. The duty concerned Krishna, the god himself, residing (for a millennium, no less!) in a shrine in Banfield. A veritable "Greek gift" for a district on the outskirts of Buenos Aires, inhabited mainly by working-class people who were too busy just getting by to devote even a small portion of their time or energy, not to mention their money, to mysticism or transcendence of any kind. Nevertheless they were compelled by an obscure superstition. So they had set up a roster for taking Krishna out on Sundays. It shouldn't have been all that hard, in principle, since there are only so many Sundays in a year, and Banfield, in the fifties, when these events occurred, already had several thousand residents. But here divine omnipotence must also be taken into account, including the power to redistribute time and its constituent quantities. This meant that at the drop of a hat the burdensome task could fall to Jusepe's family, and they would be facing a "lost Sunday": that was the most frequent of the many complaints, curses and recriminations that arose from the general grumpiness on those occasions. The father, who was always in charge, took charge of the complaining as well, since he felt more entitled than the others to complain: he was busting a gut all week in a soul-destroying job for a miserable wage and on Sunday, the only day when he might have been able to enjoy life just a little—he wasn't asking much—he had to spend the whole afternoon airing that horrible Hindu scarecrow ... through no fault of his own! Without any kind of reward, unless you believe in fairy tales (and not even then)! It had never occurred to him that there was a touch of poetic justice or injustice to all this, since Sunday's special status as a day of rest was also due to a religious superstition, and in the end there wasn't much to choose between one fictional god and another. As for taking it out on his family, he did have a kind of justification, because the individuals designated for the civic duty of promenading Krishna were fathers of boys aged between eight and twelve. Of his sons, Jusepe was the one who fell into that category; the twins were younger. This system had been arrived at by trial and error, given the local community's ignorance concerning the god in question. Krishna's appearance was enough to disconcert anyone: a kind of dwarf, he had the height and build of a schoolboy, the pale skin of a baby, which set off the shine of his big dark almond eyes, an outsize nose, and a totally incongruous mustache, with upward-pointing waxed tips. His iridescent saris looked as if they came from a toy store, while his boots by contrast were Western, Victorian, dusty, and worn with undone laces as if he had found them in the garbage. His attire, completed by plastic bracelets and necklaces, was a mere eccentricity compared to his behavior, which combined an unfortunate sense of humor with the most exasperating puerility. This manner, so at odds with the conventional image of a deity, explained why the duty had been assigned to families with boys about as old as the holy guest appeared to be: the idea was that he would have someone to entertain him.

The arrangement was superfluous. He entertained himself, although at the expense of others. Or perhaps his entertainment was provided by the world (that is, Banfield, since he never left the district). He and the world seemed to blend into one other, to judge by how, in the course of those outings, he was constantly pointing at everything, as if amazed and wanting to share his amazement. A tree, a house, a dog, a car, some boys playing ball, a police sentry box, a cloud ... Nothing escaped his jubilant pointing, fueled by an excitement that knew no moderation or nuance. He also made the inexistent appear, in garish colors, with overly sharp outlines. To be with Krishna was to become acutely aware of how many things there are in the world; after a few minutes it became overwhelming. Putting up with him for a whole afternoon could be torture. The pointing was accompanied by a ceaseless holding forth, for each thing had its name, and each name gave rise to what must have been (had anyone been able to understand them) puns, jokes, verses, and snatches of song, all of which made Krishna (and no one else) shriek with laughter. Everyone ended up with a headache.

Jusepe's father had an old Renault Dauphine, which the family could just squeeze into: the mother in front with the twins on her lap; the father at the wheel, concentrating and gritting his teeth to hold back curses that occasionally slipped out;

Jusepe and Krishna in the back. The god was always moving from one side to the other, or leaning forward to point at something through the windscreen. His constant yammering filled the little car, and as he shifted about, climbing over Jusepe, who tried to make himself small, the sari released waves of a spicy scent, which although not unpleasant in itself intensified the general unease. Jusepe felt vaguely responsible for the situation, and tried desperately to make it seem normal by looking at the things that Krishna pointed out and assuming polite (and unappreciated) expressions of gratitude and amazement. Some of those things might have interested him, like the hundred peacocks fanning their tails that the god made appear in the top of a tree, or the magnificent tiger that dissolved into a swirl of fallen leaves; but the effect was spoiled by Krishna's annoying, high-pitched voice, his bursts of uncalled-for laughter and his dizzying gesticulation. The most ill-mannered child could not have caused such a degree of mental fatigue.

This test of patience lasted all Sunday afternoon, from two or three until sundown, and sometimes later. The ugly incubus so enjoyed the outings that he tried to make them last as long as possible, and wasn't short of cunning when it came to finding underhand ways of achieving that goal. One of his ploys deeply wounded Jusepe.

On Sunday evenings, the family would be free when the caretakers of the shrine returned at last. They were an old couple who had accepted the post on the condition that they would have Sunday afternoons off, without fail. It wasn't much

of a shrine, just an old tumbledown house, which the municipality had granted to that pair of poor retirees in return for
looking after the god. It was said that they shut him up in a dark
room from Monday to Saturday, which was probably true; that
would have explained the outburst of excitement every Sunday.
As night began to fall, Jusepe's father would head to the caretakers' neighborhood, one of the most run-down in Banfield, and
drive the Renault around the block, passing in front of their
house, on the lookout for their return, so that he could be rid of
his unwelcome passenger as soon as possible. In spite of having
been out for hours, the god remained as loud and energetic as
ever; he went on driving everyone crazy, and by this point the
family would be fainting with exasperation and migraines. But
it wasn't always clear whether the old couple were there or not.
They, too, wanted peace, and as well as staying out for as long
as they could, they would leave the shutters open when they returned and not switch on the lights, in the hope that this would
be misleading, and give them a slightly longer break.

Once (Jusepe could never remember whether this really
happened "once" or on several occasions), after going past the
house two or three times without seeing any change, Jusepe's
father parked the car and sent him to see if the door was open;
it was the only way to know if the caretakers had come back:
when the old couple went out, they locked it, and when they
were at home, they left it open because the shrine was a public
building (though no one ever went there). As instructed, the
boy got out of the car. Krishna got out too and went ahead.

He gripped the doorknocker in his white, chubby little hand with painted nails, banged it vigorously, as he did everything, and turned around with a broad smile, opening his arms resignedly, and shouting something that might have meant: "No, they're not back yet; we can go on driving around." Straight away, he started back toward the car, jumping and dancing, swirling his brightly colored sari, and jingling all his bracelets in the gray, livid silence of that poor neighborhood. Jusepe followed him. But before he could take his seat in the car again, his father turned around, called him a "brainless moron," and sent him back to carry out the order that he had been given: to see whether the door was open or not. He didn't understand. Hadn't they tried and seen that it was locked? His father had to repeat himself, which intensified his anger a hundredfold. Jusepe went to see: it was open. Krishna had fooled him by using the knocker but not pushing the door. Now it yielded to Jusepe, opening to reveal the old caretaker's wife in the dark corridor, with a sour look on her face. Once rid of the annoying god, Jusepe's father gave his anger free rein. How had he ended up with such an idiot for a son, suckered so easily by that pint-sized oriental good-for-nothing! How gullible would you have to be, how pathetic, how retarded! And the recriminations went on and on; in Jusepe's mind, they would never stop. It was paradoxical: being tricked by a god should have been excusable; many of the finest philosophers have forgiven themselves the same mistake. And yet at the same time it was more unforgiveable than being tricked by a mortal.

I TOOK A STEP BACK AFTER HUGGING ENRIQUE, SO AS not to get any wetter. I was about to say that I hadn't recognized him at first, and was mentally preparing a comment or a joke about the dousing that he had received, when something else happened. As I stepped back after the hug, I probably tilted my head to one side, to get a better a look at him and come out with my joke or comment. In fact, the hug itself was already a comment on the accident, a gesture of moral support at a difficult moment since, having seen each other at breakfast a few hours earlier, it wouldn't normally have made much sense to hug him so demonstratively. In any case, by tilting my head I must have cleared a line of sight for Enrique, and what he saw seemed to catch his attention. I didn't need to turn around. I could see him gazing past me and responding with a clear look of recognition to the sound of a woman's voice. The sound of her voice, not her words, which were indistinct. But when I heard what he cried out, it was no surprise that he had been able to recognize the speaker without needing to know what she had said.

"Mama!"

Then I did turn around. At the table next to the one where Leticia and I had been sitting a few moments before was an elegantly dressed older woman, whose expression of surprise was rapidly giving way to a grin of hilarity. Her companion, a lady seated facing her, didn't seem know what was going on and was now turning around to see. Enrique's mother wasted no time explaining; she was already getting to her feet and approaching her motionless son:

"Enrique!"

As well as recognition there was a very motherly tone of affectionate scolding in her voice, as if to say: "Hasn't seen his mother for months and he turns up drenched, all dripping wet: just the sort of crazy, ridiculous thing that would happen to my son."

MANY YEARS BEFORE, ENRIQUE'S MOTHER HAD BEEN found dead, murdered, in the boot of a car, with five gunshot wounds to the face, arranged like the dots on the face of a die: one at each corner and one in the middle. Her hands and feet were tied, but there were no cuts or scratches or bruises. A neat job. The story was all over the papers for two reasons. The first was the arrangement of the shots, indicating that this was a mafia crime, with a "message." That mysterious "five" showed that the homicide was not an end in itself: it also conveyed a warning or a threat. And even if only a few initiates, who remained as elusive as the perpetrators, could "read" the message, the public as a whole became fixated on how to decipher it. The sign exercised a fascination.

But the second reason overshadowed the first, as the present overshadows the past, especially if it is an astonishing, urgent present in which each minute counts. The supposed corpse was actually no such thing. The woman was alive: by a miracle she had survived the shots, all five of which, although not of high caliber, had deeply penetrated the cranial cavity. Her life had hung by a thread for the three days she spent in the boot of that car abandoned in the woods near Ezeiza and eventually found by some cyclists. She was rushed to the best hospital in the capital and operated on by eminent surgeons. Her condition improved, and for weeks no one talked about anything else. Medical reports were released to the journalists twice a day. Because of the time differences, the international agencies were sending dispatches every half hour. The bullets were extracted one by one in separate operations. But when the fourth was being removed, it became apparent that the patient's heart would not withstand the fifth and final extraction: a transplant was imperative. By that time, advances in surgery had made heart transplants feasible and even relatively safe. The operation was a routine one, or would have been if not for the scarcity of donors, which meant that there was a long, nationwide waiting list of patients, some on life support. If Enrique's mother had been put at the end of the list she would have had to wait for months, but in her condition, without the transplant she had only hours to live. No one on those lists, of course, was going to step aside willingly. The public demanded an exception; they were clamoring for her to be given the first available heart. This was an effect of the media outcry; there was really no reason other than morbid curiosity to privilege her case, in spite of which reasons were sought and found: for example, the patient's survival was essential for solving the mystery; her evidence would bring down that dangerous mafia gang, which was a threat to public safety. The argument was utterly specious. It was objected, quite reasonably, that for the moment the mafia gang was a mere hypothesis based on little more than the pattern of the shots. Neither was it obvious that the mafia was such a danger to decent, upstanding citizens who kept their noses clean. The mafiosi killed each other. If this crime had been a settling of scores, there must have been something to settle. Were they going to save someone who was probably a criminal, and sacrifice others who were waiting anxiously for a new heart, including children, adolescents, and young mothers, many already in induced comas, with only days to live unless the operation could be carried out? The families of the patients took to the streets, blocking the traffic and causing chaos; they surrounded the hospital in a show of condemnation. But the transplant was rushed through, and days later, with the patient's new heart beating healthily, the surgeons removed the fifth bullet, which was lodged just behind the bridge of cartilage between the ethmoidal sinuses.

From that point on, the medical reports became less frequent. The patient began to recover but slowly, and when the judge was finally able to interview her, the story had almost been forgotten; the papers barely reported her statement, which was a complete anticlimax in any case: she didn't know anything. They couldn't force her to know. And she was telling the truth, or at least that's what the judge believed. The conclusion was that it had been a mistake; the intended victim was somebody else. Far from shutting the story down, this renewed the controversy. Most of the public were unconvinced. There was a deeply held belief that mafia hit men never got it wrong. But to appeal to that belief was to beg the question, since no reliable evidence had confirmed the involvement of the mafia. Besides, that idea was based on another, which was deeper and older: fundamentally, everyone is guilty. Beyond these preconceived ideas, the speculation continued. Granting that the woman had been mistaken for another, the question was: How had the mistake been made? Perhaps it was due to an extraordinary resemblance between this innocent housewife without the slightest link to the world of organized crime and the woman they had been planning to kill. In that case, who was their target? She wasn't necessarily Argentine; she could have been from anywhere. Because of the globalization of illicit business, the ease of travel in the modern world, and the extreme caution that had to be exercised by those with a mafia price on their heads, it was highly likely that the intended victim had originally lived in a remote country or continent, even in the antipodes. Fleeing to the ends of the earth was actually a necessity: the hit men were so relentless that their targets had to go to ground as far away as possible. Or rather: as *well* as possible, which didn't necessarily mean far away. Perhaps it was better to stay very close; perhaps the height of cunning was to hide in plain view, like the "purloined letter," where nobody would think to look. Although that might have been pushing it, since trying to be clever is always risky.

The families of the patients on the waiting list, who were fuming, took to the streets again to protest, carrying placards with pictures of their loved ones: victims of a capricious public opinion corrupted by sensational TV reporting.

But the journalists persisted. The media had to admit that if they stuck to the "mistaken identity" theory, the woman's declaration would be no help in solving the mystery. But the theory could still be valid; if the criminals had got confused, it must have been because of a resemblance, so the wounded woman was the clue that would lead them to the designated victim, and finding *that* woman would blow it all open.

There was a hitch, however: resemblances are facial above all, and since the victim had taken no less than five shots to the face, and subsequently undergone reconstructive surgery, it was hard to believe that her physiognomy would not have been altered. When she was discharged from hospital and resumed her interactions with friends and relatives, opinions were divided. There were those who said that she was just the same and hadn't changed at all; others found her unrecognizable; and in between these two groups was a third, for whom she was simultaneously the same and different. Appearances being so subjective, there was no way to settle the disagreement.

In a sense, this episode marked the end of professional life for Enrique's mother. She was still young, a little over fifty, but she had entered the workforce at a very early age, and by a curious coincidence, another case of mistaken identity had enabled that premature entry.

This earlier mistake had not been due to a physical resemblance, but to her name. Her family owned a big medical firm, which received a visit from the judicial police because of some dubious financial management, and the whole board of directors was arrested, including the chairwoman, a venerable octogenarian, mentally impaired by Alzheimer's disease, who had continued in the position thanks to the deference of her daughters and sons-in-law, and whose illness had facilitated the above-mentioned mismanagement. Since it was one of those traditional families in which the same first names were repeated from generation to generation, Enrique's mother, who was barely more than a girl at the time, shared her name with the old lady, who was her great-grandmother. Communicating via their lawyers, her jailed uncles ordered her to use this coincidence to occupy the vacant chair of the board. No one would know that there had been a change, because none of the previous directors were left: those who hadn't been arrested had escaped to other countries; and nobody at the next level down knew the directors (who communicated with their subordinates exclusively via typed memos). This policy of impermeable levels had been adopted years before in order to cover the draining of funds.

The young woman obeyed; she was just fourteen years old. For the next forty years, she managed the firm. All the rest of the family went into exile, with the excuse that their honor had been besmirched but in fact to enjoy their stolen wealth far from prying eyes. Oddly, despite the systematic embezzlement to which the firm had been subjected, it continued to function smoothly, thanks to the nature of its operations.

Much more intriguing, for the few who were able to observe this process, was how a young girl with no experience and very limited knowledge could handle, all on her own, the administration, management and daily running of a such a big business. She was in charge of nearly four thousand employees, working in a hundred-and-twenty-hectare processing plant (the largest in South America), and two hundred clinics throughout the country.

And yet there was no mystery—quite the opposite in fact. Precisely because she knew nothing about how companies work, the young woman confined herself to following the rules. She did this blindly, making no attempt to understand what it was all about. With each step that she had to take, she would first consult the corresponding entry in the manual and follow the instructions. She never allowed her own thinking to intervene in any way: she acted like an automaton. This wasn't very hard for her, not hard at all, in fact: she was not naturally inclined to exercise her intelligence. Not that she was stupid; in later life, years after retiring, she would demonstrate her considerable mental capacities. But back then she was still suffering from the effects of her upbringing: a rich girl, neglected by her parents and living in a superficial world, she had been deprived of intellectual stimulation.

That automatic work, performed in a sleepwalking daze, absorbed her and turned her into a loner. Her sex life began late but was clamorous and chaotic, as if she were expressing herself in a foreign language. It ended as abruptly as it had begun, and then, as she approached old age, her life became quite normal. In those few years of hormonal activity, she married one man, had a child (Enrique) with another, and got divorced, in that order.

The normal phase turned out to be short-lived, too: it was interrupted by the brutal attack that made her briefly famous, after which she had to start building a new normality from scratch. Her friends often told her that she was lucky, in the end, to have lived a series of different lives: the coddled, ignorant rich girl; the hard-working, efficient businesswoman; the tumultuous lover; normal woman "number one"; the famous mafia victim; and finally normal woman "number two." The series was discontinuous, unpredictable, erratic. Her friends found all this exciting. They'd had one life, and that was it! Actually, they felt as if they hadn't lived at all. Enrique's mother energetically rejected this dubious admiration. What the apparent multiplicity meant, she said, was that she hadn't had a *real* life (which is singular by definition).

But she preferred not to explain herself too much; in any case she couldn't, because everything pertaining to the transitions from one phase to the next was cloaked in an unreality that clouded her thinking. For reasons that remained unclear to her, she traced this confusion back to an incident that had occurred when she was a young mother: an insignificant event, slightly absurd but not so bizarre as to be a source of trauma. She knew from reading pop psychology articles in women's magazines

that giving birth could often induce a feeling of unreality. She
thought that perhaps in her case that feeling had been delayed.
The event in question had occurred one Christmas, when Enrique was a boy. She had gone to buy a new tree, since their old
one had caught fire the previous Christmas. She didn't really
know what kind she wanted, so she went to a store that she had
seen the previous day on Avenida Santa Fe, where there would
be a range to choose from: it was a very big place, with gifts at the
front and, down at the back, an enormous variety of little plastic
trees of all shapes, colors and sizes. But when she got there the
power had failed, as it often did in the big city when all the air
conditioners came on to combat the summer heat, and the grid
was under stress. There were people inside all the same. The
light coming in through the windows at the front made it possible to see the shelves of gifts, but toward the back of the store the
darkness deepened, especially for those who had just stepped
in from the harsh, white, pupil-shrinking glare of midday on the
twenty-fourth of December in Buenos Aires. Enrique's mother
asked the staff if they were open for business, and was told that
she could buy whatever she liked. They weren't at all disturbed
by the lack of power. On the contrary, they were happy: since
the registers monitored by the taxation office were out of action, they had an excuse for selling goods without receipts and
avoiding value added tax. The blackout was a godsend, coming
just at the time of year when sales were reaching their peak. Enrique's mother hesitated, but knew that she really had no choice:
it was her fault. Having left this purchase to the last minute, she

now had to face up to the shadows. She advanced toward the back of the store, between rows of plastic blue spruces, the gloom thickening steadily around her, relieved here and there by brushstrokes of a silvery subterranean gray ... Soon she entered total darkness.

Enrique's mother stretched out her arms. Her hands plunged into masses of soft needles, and when she tried to get a grip, her fingers closed on branches that pivoted up and down with a rustling sound. Gradually she began to find her bearings in that artificial forest and recognize the various kinds of synthetic pines and firs with her fingertips, telling them apart by their height and foliage. It must have been how blind people chose their Christmas trees, she thought. In spite of a vague anxiety, she persisted in her search, sensing that it would lead to a reward. In the end she decided on a tree, but when she picked it up there were two. And when she chose again, although the tree seemed to have the right size and texture, it was standing upside down. Was her sense of touch misleading her? Or were there Christmas trees in the shape of an inverted cone, with the base at the top? Perhaps, she thought, some had been hung from the ceiling because there wasn't enough space on the floor. That would have explained the hollow mother-of-pearl stars that kept brushing her forehead, supported by nothing, like real stars.

How contradictory, she thought that night as she looked at the tree set up in the living room of her apartment, sparkling with multicolored lights that flashed on and off in cheerful alternating winks. She had extracted it from the darkness. She didn't regret the purchase, because it had been an odd and memorable experience of the kind that leaves a very precise impression. Perhaps that was the only way, she thought, to enrich one's life.

Nor was there anything to regret, since it was a very handsome and sturdy little tree that served for many Christmases without the needles fading or the hinges giving out. But there must have been something strange about it, a trace of its origin, because although she never told anyone the story of how she had bought it, when people came to her apartment at Christmas, they would always pause to look at that tree with a curious expression, and quite a few made some remark along the lines of: "Objects have souls too."

This was the only episode that came back to her whenever she tried to sum up her past life, although she supposed, and with good reason, that many others must have been recorded somewhere in her memory. It must have been a kind of shorthand, one event standing in for all the rest. But it could not have been randomly chosen: the recollection must have been special in some way, like all the others, of course.... If that was where the meaning of life lay, it was very mysterious, because no two episodes can have precisely the same significance.

Her brush with the mafia, in spite of its horror, had left a less vivid mnemonic trace than the blind purchase of a Christmas tree. But neither of these episodes could halt the reconstruction of normality, whose crowning moment was the encounter in front of El Gallego with her drenched and motionless son, so touching in his bewilderment and adolescent fear of ridicule. Seeing Enrique like that made his mother realize, paradoxically, that he was an adult, with a life of his own: now she could relax and enjoy the years to come.

She was a strong woman; there was no doubt about that. She had overcome every obstacle. The firm had been shut down and dismantled years before. Its equipment and products, once recognized as groundbreaking in the field of noninvasive treatment, had been rendered obsolete by new diagnostic methods. Enrique's mother wound up the operations, duly paid out the staff, and sold the valuable sites once occupied by the plants. She retired to her elegant apartment on Avenida del Libertador and began a life of orderly leisure: reading, Pilates, movies, seeing friends and tending the garden of her country house to the north of the capital. She made a clean break with the work that had occupied her for so many years. It was no great wrench, none at all in fact, since the job had dropped into her lap as a result of a familial and legal misadventure, and she had done it conscientiously but without any sense of vocation or real interest. A trusted accountant looked after the capital that was left after the liquidation, and reported to her twice a year (in December and April).

She had kept no documents from the firm; they had all been destroyed, except for those held by various departments, ministries, commissions, and taxation authorities. Nor had she kept any souvenirs from her office; the thought had never occurred to her. And the possibility would not even have crossed

her mind, had she not been asked about it by some former employees of the firm who began to visit her a year or two after
the closure. The first phone call came as a surprise. True to
her traditional approach, she had maintained the strict isola-
tion of senior management (that is, herself), as instituted by
her uncles. So she had barely interacted with her subordinates.
But over a period of so many years, she inevitably got to know
a certain number of executives and managers and would ex-
change greetings with them, and even ask about their families.
She was a naturally courteous woman, with exquisite manners
and the scrupulous rectitude with which she always treated the
staff would have been enough to earn their lasting esteem. So
it was not implausible that they should express the desire to
say hello, to see her again, and talk about old times. The solici-
tor Gutiérrez, who had been a pillar of the firm's administrative team, made the call and assured her most politely that they
didn't want to bother her or waste her time. It was just that, a
while back, a number of former employees, all now comfortably retired, had begun to get together regularly, maintaining
the friendships that had started at the office, and they were having such fun chatting and sharing happy memories that they
had thought of inviting her to come along to one of their meetings. With a gratifying kindness, he added that she was continually present in their thoughts, as she had always been in their
working lives: a distant, discrete presence, but cherished all the
more for that. Personally, the chairwoman had no memories of
her years at the firm to share and enjoy, and in the brief interval

that had passed since the closure, the names and faces of these employees who seemed to remember her with such affection had all become a blur. She agreed to see them more for their sake than for hers. When she found out that there were only five in the group, she invited them to her apartment. The atmosphere at the meeting was pleasant. The chairwoman had told them to bring their wives, but the five men turned up on their own: they explained to her, jokingly, that it was a "men's club," and expanded on this point in the course of the conversation. The medical firm was a very old and conservative organization, they explained, and it had not appointed women to managerial positions; by the time other businesses started doing so, Enrique's mother was already chairing the board, and her long incumbency was characterized by an absolute resistance to change. Not that they meant to imply any criticism, they were quick to add, on the contrary: that timelessness had given the firm the feel of an enchanted kingdom, a world apart, and they remembered it now as the place where they had spent the best days of their lives. Yes, the employees had all been men, and at the center of the labyrinth, in the inaccessible holy of holies, the chair was occupied by a girl, who then became a woman (a beautiful woman, they gallantly said), without ever losing her air of mystery: she was like a protective deity in whom they could all trust. This mystical simile might have seemed a little far-fetched, but not to them, so consistently precise and timely were the instructions that had issued from her office. As if by some supernatural means she had always known what to do and when and how, every time, without ever making a mistake.

These compliments, which the chairwoman accepted with a slightly bored smile, were leading up to her visitors' real and hidden objective, which came to light gradually, over successive conversations, for they managed to keep finding new pretexts to meet with her. They proceeded very discreetly, by subtle moves, approaching the issue with a caution that revealed how important it was to them, without giving anything away.

What they were after was the Manual that the chairwoman had used in her work. As already mentioned, when she took over the management of the firm at the age of fourteen, without any kind of preparation or knowledge of administrative procedures, she had relied entirely on the Manual, following its instructions. She had consulted it without fail, for every task that she had to perform, large or small, crucial or trivial, from filling out a receipt to negotiating deals for raw materials with suppliers in Asia. The only skills required of her were those of basic literacy, because the instructions given by the Manual were very detailed and step-by-step. And she trusted what she read there implicitly, with the naïve trust of a child at first, then out of habit, and because experience had shown how trustworthy it was. This meant that when she retired, after successfully presiding over a large company for decades, she knew not a whit more about how a business works than when she had begun; the upside was that she never made a bad decision.

The chairwoman had not divulged the existence of the Manual. Not because she wanted to hide anything but because, in her ignorance, she had assumed that all executives and businesspeople possessed such a volume, and used it in the same way to do their jobs. The mystery existed only for the others, and it preoccupied the entire staff from the first to the last moment of her tenure. How was it possible for a young girl, who hadn't even finished secondary school, to step into the role of chair, and the very next day, without asking for advice or help from anyone, start giving the most appropriate directives? And how did she go on doing this without a false step throughout her career? None of them dared to ask her, and later they came to regret it, because she would have answered quite candidly. So they arrived at the existence of a Manual by deduction, and imagined it in elaborate detail over such a long time that it came to assume the proportions of a myth. After much deliberation, the five former employees had resolved to get hold of it.

The story that they had told the chairwoman about meeting to share memories of their years at work and revive the camaraderie of the office was a white lie: what had really brought them together was the desire to obtain the Manual, and their conversations were not in the least nostalgic; they were all about strategies for achieving their goal. They had convinced themselves, almost from the start, that the chairwoman was their only hope, which was why they had to proceed with extreme caution: there was no Plan B. At the same time they couldn't afford to move too slowly, because they feared that they were not alone in searching for that precious grail. They were wrong there, but the mistake was understandable. In their minds (in the collective mind that had conceived their plot), the Manual had taken on the aura of a magical object, which would endow its possessor with supernatural powers. They had deduced that it was a book, and therefore ideally suited to that role, since the book is the first and last key to civilization. The whole of western culture had been built on belief in the magical powers of the book. It hadn't occurred to the former employees that the magic conveyed by the Manual might be of the most unremarkable kind, suited only to solving bureaucratic problems: the magic of an efficiency that should have gone universally unnoticed. They put their faith in an intuition: the Manual of Office Work would, by virtue of its very essence, open out into the all-purpose Manual, or at least show them how to find it.

When, after the most elaborate beating about the bush, they finally broached the subject, the chairwoman confessed absently: Yes, she remembered the Manual; it had been very helpful. They held their breath. What had become of it? She shrugged her shoulders. She didn't know. As soon as the liquidation was finished and the Manual was no longer needed, she had forgotten all about it. Had she followed the Manual's instructions in winding up the firm? Surprised by the question, she said yes: how else could she have done it? She hadn't known then, and still didn't, what a liquidation was and how it worked, much less how to liquidate such a vast and complex organization. Shivers ran through the bodies of the five men as she said this. They felt that they were finally touching the mystery with their fingertips.

Treading warily, like hunters trying not to startle an exceptionally timid deer, they pursued their questioning. The chairwoman remembered that when, summoned by her uncles, she had first set foot in the offices of her predecessor, she had found them deserted and in a mess, with open boxes and papers on the floor: the debris of evidence destroyed in a hasty evacuation. In a recess, down at the back, there had been a shelf with some books on it, not many: they looked like encyclopedias and catalogues ... That's where the Manual had been, she thought, she was almost sure, but on its own, apart from the rest; she had found it on the first day, in the first hour, and hadn't even looked at the other books. Yes, she had taken it to her desk, because she consulted it continually, but before going home in the evening she would put it back on one of those shelves. So she supposed that in the last hour of the last day, she had returned it to that spot. She couldn't really remember, but that seemed the most likely scenario. And from that point on, she told them again, she had never given the Manual another thought, until they reminded her of it.

Had she been so sure that she would never need it again? Apparently she had been.

As for what had happened to the Manual after that, she could only presume that it had been included, along with the other books and the furniture, in one of the lots put up for sale at the time ... No, she couldn't give them any precise information about the sale. She wasn't even sure that there had been one. Once the site of the central plant had been sold, she had

stepped right back; the buildings, which were decrepit and im-
practical, were only worth the materials that could be stripped
from them (tower blocks had been built on the site, and a shop-
ping mall, and tanks for the overflow from Laguna Cochina).
The most likely scenario was that the few usable pieces of furniture from the offices had ended up in a secondhand store.

And the books? Might someone have contacted a secondhand book dealer? The chairwoman didn't think so. There
weren't that many. Twenty or thirty, she guessed, nicely bound;
she couldn't reveal anything about their content because she
had never opened them.

And the Manual? What did it look like?

Well, the Manual wasn't bound. It had a soft cover, but it
must have been coated with plastic or treated with some sub-
stance that toughened it, and very effectively, since it had managed to withstand all those years of constant use without falling
apart. She couldn't tell them anything about the color or design
of the cover: it was hidden by the film of plastic, or whatever it
was. What she went on to say left them totally flabbergasted: It
wasn't a very thick book.

They asked her about the title and the author. In vain. The
cover was illegible, because of the film; she always went straight
to the part she needed to consult and never bothered to look
at the title page. At this point, Enrique's mother must have realized that she wasn't being much help with what, to them,
was clearly a matter of great importance, and she apologized,
explaining that when an object is so useful, when you need it

so often and for such specific purposes, you don't really have much time to contemplate its physical characteristics. Observing things in that way requires a detachment and a distance that had never entered into her dealings with the Manual.

As to how it was organized, how you looked things up, whether it had indexes and diagrams, whether it was arranged alphabetically or was a kind of step-by-step primer, her answers were vague, noncommittal and began to drift dangerously toward fatigue and irritation. On the first occasion the men didn't insist, and when later on they tried other angles, for example mentioning a specific problem to find out how she had looked up the solution, they didn't have any more luck. In the end, they came to believe that she really couldn't remember.

One thing she could confirm was that the book had been printed. Which eliminated a possibility that had been worrying them: that it was a manuscript, or a typescript, which would have meant that its loss was irreparable. However rare a printed book is, there will always be more than one copy ... But this was not much consolation when they remembered those stories about bibliophiles taking decades to track down a rare book, even though they had a description and publication details; the former employees, by contrast, were hunting a ghost.

In their follow-up meetings, the five went over all the questions, the answers, the digressions (which were long and frequent, and necessary if they were not to come across as monomaniacs and frighten or distress the chairwoman). They analyzed every word that she had pronounced, with its intonation and accompanying gestures or facial expressions. Likewise, they conferred about the apartment, the elegant living room in which the meetings took place, the adjacent dining room, which they looked into occasionally, pretending to admire the pictures, and the hallway that led to the bathroom, which, given the condition of their respective prostates, they could plausibly frequent, discreetly peering into various rooms along the way. They had not initially ruled out the possibility that the Manual might be somewhere in the apartment. But they soon did, along with the rest of their suspicions. They came to believe that the chairwoman was sincere. No, they had not fallen into a trap laid by a cunning sorceress. Comparing their observations in long sessions of debriefing left no doubt in their minds.

As much as they talked and thought things over, they couldn't make head or tail of the case. They had to admit that it had been the almost impossible strangeness of it all that had attracted them in the first place, but it was no less true that the impossibility had remained and was indeed deepening. How could a book provide all the answers? That, in itself, verged on the inexplicable, even if the *all* in question was limited to business management. In fact, that was not such a strict limitation, because managing a business raises a very broad range of questions beyond the domains of economics and accounting. Not only had the book provided all the answers, more inexplicably still, it had gone on doing so for four decades, as if nothing had changed; and those years, from the 1960s to the 1990s, had been a time of great turbulence, for Argentina and the world. The conditions in which the business operated at the end of that period would have been unimaginable at the start.

So the answers could not have been spelled out literally; that was out of the question. The men had to consider other possibilities, and the only one that occurred to them was that the answers had been produced by some kind of combinatory system. They tried to imagine how it could work. One advantage of this hypothesis was that it explained the dimensions of the volume, which were modest, according to the chairwoman. Combinatorics was the most effective means of compression. You only had to think of the thousands of different sequences that could be produced by reordering a set of ten elements. A relatively small book could contain enough components to generate a virtually infinite number of combinations.

But of course, to make use of such a system, you would need to have a key. And they could not imagine that nice lady possessing such occult knowledge, not even now, in her retirement, much less when she had taken charge of the firm. All their investigations indicated that, right from the start, all she had needed to do to "read" the Manual was open it. That could only mean that the key was something natural, already lodged in the brain. And if the key really worked, it could be used to decode books of any kind, not just handbooks. Puzzled, far more puzzled than at the outset of their quest, the five men came to the conclusion that all books were the Manual, and that everyone possessed the key with which to find instructions in them, fail-safe instructions for what to do and how to succeed in life.

ENRIQUE HADN'T MOVED; THE COLD, CRYSTALLINE WA-
ter was still streaming off him. The accident had frozen his slim
form before us, as if a magic ray, a lustral ray of liquid, had im-
mobilized a single story in the midst of the unstoppable flow:
the storyless story of the youth of Palermo Soho.

Let us take advantage of this frozen moment to sketch in the
spatial and temporal background. After long decades of poverty, stagnation and decadence, Argentina had entered a phase
of prosperity. The economy had ceased to be a problem; no
one had to worry about how to pay the bills; they paid themselves, by direct debit. Money, the proverbial scarce good, had
become plentiful, even to excess, which had surprised everyone
and stunned not a few. Since all the beneficiaries of this trans-
formation had already been living comfortably (the poor, of
course, went on being poor), what distinguished the situation
was the provision of "extras." Many people who didn't really
need to work were busy creating superfluous necessities, selling
and distributing goods to satisfy them, and thereby harvesting
handsome profits. These, in turn, were immediately spent on
hedonistic consumption. The formerly backward and provin-
cial nation was brashly making up for the years it had spent re-
senting the triumph of the First World. Voices of caution were

heard now and then, pointing out that the trade surplus and the financial surplus were bubbles sustained only by commodity prices, and that when those prices fell, the bubbles would pop just like that. No one listened, and for once they were right. China's economic rise had barely begun, and all the indications were that it would continue for at least a century. Given that forecast, the vast dimensions and population of the oriental giant imposed a change of perspective. It was estimated that when China attained its full development, three planets the size of the Earth would be required to satisfy its demand for consumer goods. This estimate suggested a transmutation of Time into Space. Three beautiful, blue Earths floating in space: not some illusory economic bubble, but three solid spheres with their seas and forests and mountains, their people and beasts, their dinosaurs and nightingales ... How would the gracious dance of those three globes affect the gravitational balance of the solar system? By then, China, the Chinas, would be full of designer stores and bar restaurants, so numerous and spread over such a large area that it would be hard to find the center. But the youth of Argentina had located it in advance, in that small district of Buenos Aires known as Palermo Soho. The center of that center, incidentally, was the place where Borges had spent his childhood and discovered literature. The games that Borges had played with space-time in his work were secondary to his art of storytelling; his presence hovered over the neighborhood where I had come to stay, and I gave thanks for the fortuitous recommendation that had led me there. Before the divorce, I had lectured on Borges in Providence, but I had read his work in translation, and many of its secrets had no doubt eluded me.

The center, for me, was Enrique's guest house. It was the radiant source of a life composed of ever-new, constantly changing images. Because of my personal circumstances, principally the sense of impermanence that followed the divorce, I had gone in search of some kind of eternity. I hadn't been aware of this at the time of choosing my destination and setting off, but over the days spent in Palermo I had begun to intuit it, and it dawned on me fully that morning. I had fled from a time that was threatening to turn my daughter into a stranger growing up far away from me. And of all the places in the world, by a stroke of luck, I had ended up precisely in the one, so far from Providence, where it was held to be impossible that commodity prices could fall. It's not surprising that I hadn't ventured beyond the magic circle of Palermo. I was realistic enough to suspect that people must have had a more matter-of-fact attitude to time in other neighborhoods of Buenos Aires. But I didn't go and find out.

A clarification is in order here, for it is hard to understand how temporal succession could be denied like this precisely where fashion was moving so quickly, setting its stamp on the passing seasons, months and days more emphatically than anywhere else. Evanescence was processed and displayed; forms, colors and functions ran a crazy sack race. The neighborhood itself could have gone out of fashion at any moment (faraway

San Telmo was threatening to supplant it). And most of the businesses were renting on short leases, which were always coming up for renewal. Time seemed to rule everything. And yet it was not so. Time was merely the mask that eternity had put on to seduce the young.

Fashion, moreover, was the only spiritualism that found favor among the Argentines, by nature a deeply agnostic, secular, masonic and skeptical people. According to a charming national superstition, the only spirits who would respond to the call of a medium were those of historically significant public figures. And given the socioeconomic determinants of Argentine history, those people invariably belonged to patrician settler families: an English-style aristocracy of elegant gentlemen, attentive to the cloth, the cut, and the care of their apparel. This was where the common people who had invented the legend exercised their gently vengeful sense of humor: however often those dandies of yesteryear were summoned, whenever they returned from their adventures beyond the grave, their trousers were torn or the lapels of their frock coats were spotted with sauce. They came back to demand new clothes. The way to deliver those clothes to the gaucho underworld was to buy them and give them to somebody poor.

The myth of the Indirect Gift infused its poetry into every commercial transaction in Palermo. But this had no visible effect on the clothing of the poor people circulating among us: the children begging for coins at the tables, the women breastfeeding their babies in doorways, the cardboard collectors. They were still wearing their traditional rags.

Among the picturesque beggars I encountered during my brief stay was an older man, not elderly, although he must have been getting there (it was hard to guess his age), who had lost a leg, the left one. It had been amputated at mid-thigh or slightly closer to the groin. Someone would set him up on a chair, on a corner, or between the entrances of two restaurants, or at some other strategic point where lots of people were passing by, and he would stay there all day. His method consisted of hailing passersby as if he had something important to say to them, making them stop and come over, and then explaining that he needed money, just a bit, whatever, even a single coin, "for the leg." He didn't go into details, but the most obvious supposition was that he was referring to a prosthetic limb. Holding his open hand vertically at a distance of twenty centimeters from the stump, he would add: "I've already saved up to here," as if he had calculated the cost of an artificial leg and its length, and divided the sum into centimeters. But he wasn't serious. One day he would put his hand five centimeters from the stump, and the next day it would be much further out, where the knee would have been, or further still. This might have been strategic: by showing that he had saved for a small portion of the leg, he might have been suggesting that his earnings were scant, that people were selfish, or that Palermo made a poor showing when it came to Christian charity ... By contrast, when he put his hand further out, perhaps it meant that people had been generous, and that he only needed a little bit more to realize his dream of walking again. He could choose one argument or the other depending on the appearance of the person he was hailing, because both approaches—"I'm way off" and "I'm nearly there"—could be effective, but with different kinds of people. I watched him for hours and came to the conclusion that he was doing it at random, which I should have known from the start, because if there had been a worked-out strategy, it would have been accompanied by coherent speech and clear diction, not that incomprehensible drunken mumbling. And in any case, all but the most unsuspecting tourists knew that he didn't save a peso but blew it all right away on cheap wine.

The spectral extension of that leg was part of a historical regime that negated negation itself. The new prosperity had served to create the Present, and fill it with luxury items and pleasurable activities. Since the Present was, by definition, so brief, it was easily filled, and there was money left over. Thus one Present could be replaced with another, and this new Present with another still, in an uninterrupted continuum, an agenda without any gaps, which young people called "enjoying life."

But time, kicked out of the front door, came back in through the window. Argentina's wealth was a mirage, not only because it depended on something as remote and unreal as China's trade balance, but also because the only wealth that people could really aspire to was that of their own history. And history and stories require a departure from the continuum of happiness. If someone had pointed this out, the youth of Palermo Soho would have asked: But how can you not be happy, even for a moment? And what is there but the moment? The atmosphere they were living in made endings inconceivable. For the Present to be fractured, one would have had to imagine a miraculous glitch, an accident involving all the atoms in the universe.

The constant consumption of pseudostories (immune to interruption by misfortune) had dulled the perception of reality. When the universe broke open and death came in through the crack, no one noticed. This situation continued until my return to Providence, and according to the Argentine press, which I consult every day on the internet, it has continued up till now. If Argentina lapsed back into poverty, it would be interesting to see if anyone noticed: a very hard experiment to run, admittedly, not to mention the fact that these things depend on how they're interpreted.

Enrique had opened up to me, in our long after-dinner conversations, when the others had gone off to bed. Like all the young people of his generation and social milieu, he had taken advantage of the sexual permissiveness of the time. Handsome, rich, endowed with a charming smile and a quick wit, he had missed no opportunity to seduce and conquer. These adventures were all destined to be brief; it was in their nature, after all. Acquiring an education in love could happily occupy a whole life ("life" here being understood as a synonym for "youth"). The succession of lessons was endless. Everything was love, but love itself was synonymous with the anticipation of love.

As for sex, a curious mental readjustment had to be made. Or rather, it had already been made. But there was a lingering feeling that one day, at some point, it might have to be reversed. Without ever putting it into words, Enrique felt that one day a young woman might say to him: "I don't sleep around" or "I have a boyfriend," or something like that. This had never happened, nor was it about to. But it was a latent possibility, like the existence of parallel worlds. And that latency had contaminated the world in which he was living, making it parallel too.

The prospect of true love graced his encounters with emotion and poetry, particularly in the case of a beautiful young woman whom he had met some months earlier, at the beginning of spring. Although there was nothing special about her, she seemed different, unique; he didn't know why. She was beautiful, but there was no shortage of beauty in the streets; nor was there anything really exceptional about her rather distant charm, or the intelligence of her repartee. She knew how to surround herself with a veil of mystery. Even after various conversations, which always began with a chance meeting in the street and continued with a coffee or a walk, Enrique hadn't learned where she came from or how she spent her time; he knew almost nothing about her. He found it intriguing that he hadn't seen her before, since in the usual Palermo circles everyone knew everyone else. And suddenly, from one day to the next, all he had to do to meet her was walk around for a while in the busiest part of the area: the streets near Plaza Serrano. Had she just moved into the neighborhood? Had she, like so many others, discovered the charms of its boutiques and bars? Had she started working nearby? This last hypothesis was the least likely, since whenever he had run into her, at any hour of the day or night, she had always been able to accept his invitation: they would go and have a drink, and talk for hours.

Conditions were favorable to lingering because, as Enrique stressed when he was telling me the story, all of this was happening at the beginning of a warm spring, which made the open air so welcoming that nobody wanted to be inside. The café terraces were full from morning. Birds thronged in the new foliage covering the trees. A sky of changeless blue showered its benevolent light on the tables where, as the hours of the day went by, the mineral water was transmuted into beer, wine, champagne, and shots of whisky, each drink with its particular hue: the gold of grain, the amber or ruby of grapes, the phosphorescent green of mint, or the iridescent red of sangria. The finely balanced dance of shadows, governed by the course of the sun, was at once leisurely and volatile; there was always something unpredictable about it, as if new stars were appearing in the firmament, before and after midday, describing sinuous, elliptical trajectories. Breezes of calibrated coolness made their stately way through the streets, like Egyptian slaves waiting on the rich, or on those who felt rich simply by virtue of being in Palermo, watching time go by. The contents of the storefront windows were refreshed: they looked like abstract pictures, with curious hints of figuration. The spring fashions had been displayed in winter, so the windows moved on to summer when spring came, competing with each other as well as keeping ahead of time. The galleries, bookstores, and ubiquitous designer stores welcomed the season of beauty in style. All the commercial, social and cultural life of Palermo flowed into the cafés, which emptied themselves onto the terraces and sidewalks, where the breezes continued their parade, and the birds sang on. It wasn't Enrique's first spring in the neighborhood, but he perceived this one with a new clarity that owed something to the presence of the beautiful young woman at his side. And she delighted in the weather and the surroundings as if for the very first time, as if witnessing the dawn of the world. That was the active ingredient in her charm.

She had come with the spring, with the first warm days, and seemed to be one with the kindness of the climate. Her clear gaze would vanish, along with her smile, into the shifting multitudes that occupied those days of good fortune. Time went by, and Enrique wondered how it was that in spite of their daily meetings and the conversations on which he had almost come to depend, he knew so little about her. It wasn't that she refused to answer his questions; he never asked her any. He forgot, he got distracted; it was enough simply to enjoy her presence, her beauty, her voice. She was mysterious, but not by design. Paradoxically, like all mysteries, she gave an impression of transparency. Her beauty was greater by night than by day. He invited her to dinner at his favorite restaurants in the area, and then, after midnight, they would have a drink on a cafe terrace, underneath the stars. Instead of trying to find out something definite, he would ask her silly questions, like: "Which do you prefer, the sun or the moon?" To which she replied, with equanimity, that she liked them both the same. He showed her around his guest house, told her about the Evolution Club and his mother and his schooling, which the fire had interrupted. He had never felt so eloquent.

As spring advanced toward summer, the poetic friendship drew closer to love. There came a day when Enrique had to admit that he was smitten. This was not the attraction or the desire that he had felt for other women; it was something special. Or rather, it was the same thing, since he had no other psychic mold to pour it into, but with the addition of Mystery. Had he fallen in love with Mystery? The Mystery that he himself had fashioned, with his reticence and fantasies? If so, this might have been a symptom of megalomania, like believing that one has been chosen or is the protagonist of a story. The way stories unfolded, he thought, should have taught him some humility. Except that it hadn't been so much an "unfolding" as a "consumption" of stories. In any case, these ruminations were suspended as soon as he saw her again. From the little he knew of Mystery, it could never have taken a form so like that of a beautiful young woman. The woman was solid, while he had always imagined Mystery to be porous. Her pale and exquisitely smooth skin reflected the light in strips of lustrous hue. He had never even touched it. An almost inanimate chasteness governed their relationship, promising sensual pleasures all the more intense for having been delayed. Gazes, more than words, conveyed their growing passion. Her eyes always had the sheen of water, but a water that was intoxicating. From a certain moment on, those eyes began to transmit a message that came directly from Mystery itself.

That was the moment at which Enrique declared his love. She showed no sign of surprise. Only a fool would not have guessed. A few days went by. He respected her silence, supposing that Mystery was at work. Finally, she told him that his feelings for her were reciprocated. Enrique lost himself in the depths of that gaze, where he felt that he would be able to find answers for which there were no questions. This happened late one night. They had been walking through the narrow streets, where people were lingering still. When she said goodbye to him, on a dark corner, they kissed. It was the first time. A brief kiss, in which their souls communicated. Although not much, it seems, because Enrique was left in a quandary that lasted several days. And he was so perplexed that he didn't dare kiss her again in that time. She was increasingly affectionate with him. It was as if Mystery had drawn near.

But the revelation, when it occurred, was an anticlimax: the mountain gave birth to a mouse. The young woman said that after thinking long and hard, she had decided to tell him who she was and what she was doing there. The decision had been difficult, and painful in a way, because it spelled the end of a situation in which she had discovered a feeling that she had thought she would never know. But thinking it over, she had

seen that it couldn't go on. She suspected that the special charm
of the situation was due to its ambiguity, and yet she had to
make things clear, she had to lay her cards on the table, or dot
the i's and cross the t's, or whatever it was that humans said in
cases like that ...

Hearing these last words, Enrique started visibly. Wasn't she
human? he asked.

By way of a reply, she smiled, as if to say: Do I seem inhu-
man to you? Do I look like an animal? A monster? An allegory?

He could only smile in turn. She was more human than anyone he had ever met. In fact, he suspected that he would, from
then on, define and measure the human in relation to her. It's
only when you're in love, he said, that you perceive the humanity of the human.

And yet ...

She began to tell her story, explaining that there were benevolent supernatural powers (to call them gods would have
been too much) who watched over well-off people pursuing
their leisure activities. The general economy of the Universe
had judged the existence of these powers to be necessary, since
the entities and deities who saw to the survival of the human
race had neither the time nor the inclination to bother with
what they considered unnecessary trifles. Trifles, true, but not
so unnecessary from the point of view of those concerned. For
example, ensuring that the heating worked on the upper floors
of hotels, that silk shirts didn't irritate the skin, or that the bubbles in champagne were small and quick, not big and sluggish.

Admittedly, compared to preventing catastrophes like earth-quakes and floods, plagues and poverty, these tasks did seem trivial. Could the fates who prevented planes from crashing care whether the seats in business class leaned back far enough or not? It had been generally felt, among the benevolent pow-ers, that attending to minor details was a distraction from the big picture. But with the advance of civilization it became clear that there were sufficient supernatural forces for everyone and everything. And so these specialized powers had gradually come into existence.

One of the matters in their charge was ensuring the supply of ice for drinks in places with warm climates or high rates of consumption. Boulevard Saint-Germain, Piazza Navona, and the East Village, for example, were on the list of supported lo-calities, to which Palermo Soho had recently been added. So as soon as the warm weather began, Enrique's friend was sent to ensure that there would be ice enough for all the drinks con-sumed in the neighborhood's various establishments. Without her, the little cubes or cylinders of ice would not have been suf-ficiently cold, or melted gradually enough, or made that charac-teristic sound when they knocked against each other. As long as she was present, no one would lack the ice they needed to cool their drink and have a good time.

How did she do it? Whether she was naturally discreet or reluctant to scare him with graphic descriptions, she didn't go into details, but she hinted that her power depended on a symbolic transfer. She was ice, or its superior and inexhaustible essence. They had given her a human form so that she would not attract attention. And it went without saying that he would have to keep what he had just heard to himself; she had already committed an offence by telling him. The kind of mission that she had been charged with was secret by its very nature.

It took Enrique a long moment to assimilate this information. The first thing that occurred to him, after mentally summarizing the case, was that his love was condemned to be a summertime romance.

And that was not the worst of it. They were condemned to keep their distance, because an embrace would be fatal to her, as she pointed out; she begged him to consider the properties of ice before getting to the stage of amorous effusions.

Could this fable have been an indirect way of telling him that she was frigid?

No, it wasn't, she wasn't. On the contrary. Hadn't he heard about how ice can burn?

For love, Enrique was ready to face the eternal, eternally burning ice of Hell.

The ice of Heaven was no less dangerous.

And so it was that my young friend embraced his beloved and she disappeared in his arms, becoming a cascade. I was ideally placed to witness this metamorphosis, which was the high point of my fortunate and instructive stay in Buenos Aires. The story did not come to a happy end, but stories rarely do. In fact, they rarely come to an end of any kind, because the teller gets tired along the way, or bored, or fears that people will make fun of him.

And anyway, how could there have been an ending if the beginning was still going on? Everything had happened in the blink of an eye. Oblivious to the accident that he had caused, El Gallego kept turning the crank handle. Enrique, like an actor left in the middle of the stage when the play has finished, stood there dripping, motionless, stunned by the surprise. And with one hand, he went on holding the delicate machine at his side: that "little steel fairy," the bicycle, from whose spinning stories are born.

MARCH 29, 2008

PRAISE FOR CÉSAR AIRA

ARTFORUM

"César Aira is an experimental Argentinian author whose short fiction is often funny and always mind-boggling. His new novella, *Artforum*, is an excellent entry point into his wild body of work." – *GQ*

"For a novella like *Artforum*, one doesn't need to reach deep into the toolkit of literary theory. Aira creates his own epistemology. It's marvelous to witness.... Aira is unencumbered. He does what he does, and what we receive is giddy, unquestionably self-indulgent, and yet absolutely perfect." – Kamil Ahsan, NPR

BIRTHDAY

"This memoir by Argentine writer Cesar Aira, written for his 50th birthday, is his strongest work to come out in a while — subtle and masterful, though very different from a lot of his other books in its intimate, more direct personal narrative. He finds an access route to the deepest regions of a passing thought without overworking anything. With Aira, you always want to go along for the ride." – Greenlight Bookstore

GHOSTS

"Exhilarating. César Aira is the Duchamp of Latin American literature. — *The New York Times Book Review*

"Aira conjures a languorous, surreal atmosphere of baking heat and quietly menacing shadows that puts one in mind of a painting by de Chirico." — *The New Yorker*

HOW I BECAME A NUN

"*How I Became a Nun* is the work of an uncompromising literary trickster." — *Time Out*

THE LINDEN TREE

"It has taken 14 years for this book to reach us in English, and that is too long to wait. We want more, and we want it yesterday." — Patrick Flanery, *Spectator*

THE LITERARY CONFERENCE

"Aira's novels are eccentric clones of reality, where the lights are brighter, the picture is sharper and everything happens at the speed of thought." — *The Millions*

THE LITTLE BUDDHIST MONK & THE PROOF

"Aira's blazing novelettes serve as a reminder (as "Proof") that there are some things that can only be pulled off in writing, and that these things can flare up and vanish in the space of 90 pages, leaving their beautiful, inexplicable ash swirling in our minds."
– Brenton Woodward, *Liminoid Magazine*

THE MIRACLE CURES OF DR. AIRA

"César Aira is indeed Dr. Aira, and the miracles are the little books he creates." – *The Coffin Factory*

THE MUSICAL BRAIN

"Aira's stories seem like shards from an ever-expanding interconnecting universe." – Patti Smith, *The New York Times*

THE SEAMSTRESS AND THE WIND

"A beautiful, strange fable ... alternating between frivolity, insight, and horror." – *Quarterly Conversation*

SHANTYTOWN

"With a few final acts of narrative sleight of hand (and some odd soliloquies) the reader is left at once dazzled and unsettled."
– *Los Angeles Times*

VARAMO

"Aira seems fascinated by the idea of storytelling as invention, invention as improvisation and improvisation as transgression, as *getting away with something.*"   – *The New York Times Book Review*

"A lampoon of our need for narrative. No one these days does metafiction like Aira."   – *The Paris Review*